DEATH IN SHEEP'S CLOTHING

STELLA PHILLIPS

WALKER AND COMPANY
NEW YORK

All the characters and events portrayed in this story are fictitious.

First published in the United States of America in 1983 by the Walker Publishing Company, Inc.

ISBN: 0-8027-5489-9

Library of Congress Catalog Card Number: 82-73569

Printed in the United States of America

10 9 8 7 6 5 4 3 2 1

CHAPTER ONE

LAURA SHANNON poured a third cup of tea from the cooling pot and glumly watched the rain drumming on the window. Beyond the window the little backyard lay in puddles, the rank shrubs dripping miserably.

Oh God, the kids won't be able to play outside, she thought, and the prospect of them bickering around her feet all day darkened her mood further.

She supposed she ought to go upstairs and see if they were still alive, nothing much less drastic than death would keep that pair in bed at nine o'clock in the morning. In fact six o'clock was more usually the hour for the merry cries to start ringing round the house. But she did not move. Four years of motherhood had instilled a deep reluctance to wake a sleeping child, and she needed the time to go over her breakfast quarrel with George. If she called the children down before she was calmer she would be screaming at them before they got to the foot of the stairs.

The house was to blame, she decided, looking round the big dark kitchen; this absurd house and the dull little town of Elmbridge. How she wished herself back in Meddenham where she had friends she could dump the children on while she went to the cinema or had a hair-do. The remembered delights of Meddenham, so much more rosy than the realities had been, brought tears to Laura's blue eyes. She recalled her bright council flat with its immaculate fitted kitchen, forgetting the high rent and the constant complaints from neighbours about the children's noise.

But George had said they must have a house in the country. They must get away from the flat and gadding out at night and start a real family life. George, as he never tired of telling her, had suffered a wretchedly unhappy childhood, dragged from pillar to post by feckless parents. When he was fourteen-years-old his parents had died within a month of each other, showing more devotion in death than they ever had in life, and he had finished his upbringing with Aunt Grace Roach. Which Laura had to concede couldn't have been any picnic.

So George had this thing about a lovely family life like you saw on the telly and so very rarely in real life. And, to be honest, she had shared his dream of the elegant house, with the big garden for the children to run wild in, and she and George having supper out on the patio when the children were tucked up in bed rosily asleep. And the only place for this dream house was in Elmbridge, a pretty little town only twelve miles from George's office in Meddenham, and so conveniently close to Aunt Grace's home. The Shannons had great expectations of Aunt Grace.

But actual house hunting in Elmbridge had brought their grandiose dreams to an abrupt halt. To begin with there was very little empty property in Elmbridge, and what there was was extremely expensive. Other families had found the town highly desirable also. And they had a lot more cash to purchase their dreams than the Shannons. In fact the Shannon's modest deposit plus the highest mortgage repayments they could possibly manage on George's salary, would only have bought them a Victorian workman's cottage with four small rooms and a tiny backyard.

Aunt Grace was the obvious answer. The Shannons were giving up their pleasant life in Meddenham they told themselves, solely to be near her in her declining years. The least she could do was to offer financial help in buying them a suitable house or, failing this, provide them with a flat in Rowan Lodge.

Rowan Lodge was Aunt Grace's house to which she had retired ten years previously when she had sold her small newspaper and sweet shop. It was the perfect family house, impressive enough to measure up to the Shannons' wildest dreams, big enough for Aunt Grace not to get underfoot. And it wasn't as if Rowan Lodge wasn't coming to George one day. Aunt Grace 'had no one else'.

But Aunt Grace, most unreasonably, had not seen it that way. She enjoyed brief well-ordered visits from the Shannons. She could criticise the children's behaviour in the teeth of Laura's fixed smile. To have them around all the time would have taken the edge off the pleasure.

And as for assistance in buying them a house, nothing that Laura would consider could be bought for under five thousand pounds. Such sums were quite beyond Aunt Grace's means. Things had been at an *impasse* when Miss Bennett, Aunt Grace's mouse-like companion, had the first original idea of her life.

Laura recalled the scene vividly. It had been during one of their Sunday visits about nine months previously. Lunch had passed reasonably amicably and they were sitting around Aunt Grace's large, over-furnished lounge. Laura, as usual, was mentally throwing out Aunt Grace's possessions and refurnishing the room to her own taste, the children were jumping about and setting the serried ranks of Aunt Grace's precious china tinkling, Aunt Grace herself sat ramrod straight in her big leather chair. Miss Bennett, knowing her place, was seated on the edge of the group, furthest from the fire, when she had suddenly said, "What about the old police station?"

"What about the old police station?" Aunt Grace had echoed.

"It's empty," Miss Bennett went on. "They've built a new one in the middle of the High Street. The council offered the old one to other local government departments but none of them wanted it, so now it's going to be open to tenders from the public."

Aunt Grace thumped the walking cane she affected on the floor a couple of times. She was a formidable figure, tall and skinny, with a strong beaked nose, dark eyes, and hair still more black than grey. Like Meg Merrilees, thought Laura, surreptitiously flicking little Judy's fingers from her nose. She always half expected Aunt Grace's stick to whack out at one of the children.

"How d'you know all this?" Aunt Grace had rasped in her deep mannish voice.

"Mr. Wainwright told me," Miss Bennett murmured. "He retired three months ago and moved in with his daughter. There's a new police sergeant now, but he has a flat above the new station."

"Got nothing better to do than gossip on my time," Aunt Grace muttered as a pure formality. Sergeant Wainwright she knew. He had visited the house on several occasions when she had seen prowlers in the garden. Aunt

Grace had a morbid fear of intruders, not without reason as shortly before she had retired she had been savagely beaten up in her shop by a youth who had departed with a week's takings. He, like the more recent prowlers, had never been apprehended, a fact that had further jaundiced her never very sweet view of human nature. "Wainwright was useless, quite useless. I hope the new man is more efficient."

"Sergeant Cantwell," supplied Miss Bennett. "They say he is very capable."

"Good. Perhaps we'll be able to sleep easier in our beds now. Well, what's it like?"

"What?" stammered Miss Bennett. She had lost the thread of conversation, a thing that quite often happened with her.

"The police station, what is it like? I can't remember." When Miss Roach had retired from her shop she had virtually retired from life. The shop had been very busy, a little gold mine George used to say, his eyes gleaming, but now she rarely went into the town and had largely lost touch with it. Such news as she heard filtered through Miss Bennett who she had recruited on the day she moved into Rowan Lodge and enslaved ever since.

"Well," said Miss Bennett, "it's got possibilities."

"You mean it's a ruin," put in George.

"Be quiet, George," Aunt Grace snapped. "I lived in two rooms above a shop for sixty years of my life and so did my parents before me. Young people nowadays expect everything before they are out of the cradle. Nice houses, motor cars, expensive holidays, things we worked a lifetime for. Speak up, Annie. What is the place like?"

"I believe it's very damp. Mrs. Wainwright was always

complaining of it. And it would need quite a lot of repairing, and complete redecoration, of course. But you could probably get it very cheaply, and there are these grants you can get from the government. Discretionary grants, they're called. Up to a thousand pounds for modernisation if you match them pound for pound."

"You mean the government actually gives away a thousand pounds, no strings attached?" Aunt Grace was really interested now.

"That's right," Laura said. "I was reading about it in a newspaper only last week. Do you think this place would be eligible for a grant, Miss Bennett?"

"Mrs. Wainwright thinks it would." Miss Bennett clasped her hands together, quite carried away at being the centre of attention. "If the news doesn't leak out that it's on the market you might get it for a few hundred pounds, and you could do wonders to it with a couple of thousand. Make a lovely place out of it."

Make a lovely place out of it, thought Laura bitterly. And yet she had to admit that on that bright spring day when she first saw the house she had been fired with its possibilities.

Ex-sergeant Wainwright had taken them on their tour of inspection. The house was quite large and nicely situated at one end of the High Street with the river and the bridge over it less than a hundred yards away. There was not the big garden the Shannons would have liked, just a small backyard with a number of half-ruined outbuildings and a high crumbling brick wall around it. But with the river and water meadows so near it was almost an extension of their grounds, and the rooms were big and nicely proportioned. Besides, it was rather quaint the way Sergeant Wainwright kept referring to 'the charge room' and 'the parade room'. When had Elmbridge had a police force big enough to parade, Laura wondered. And the two cells were very cute, with built-in bunks, and high barred windows, and great thick doors with hatches to push the food through, and dear little peep-holes with moveable covers. The Shannons had thought the cells would make a wonderful talking point, and while Sergeant Wainwright conscientiously explained the ancient wiring and the pre-historic plumbing, their minds had been winging away through *Homes and Gardens* to their finished chic abode.

"We'll turn the cells into bedsitter studies for the children when they're older," said George.

"And we'll get one of those antique front doors with plastic hinges," she had joined in, "and a carriage lamp beside the door."

"No, a blue lamp!" They had giggled and held hands and run on ahead of the ponderous old policeman who couldn't see what was so marvellous about the house he and his wife had been so heartily glad to get out of.

"We'll call it Blue Lamp Cottage."

"Clink Cottage!"

"No," George's plump and pompous face went solemn. "We'll call it The Old Station House."

Laura got up stiffly from the breakfast table and started clearing the dishes across to the sink. What had gone wrong, she wondered. When had the dream died? She put the food away in the pantry and looked at the dishes without enthusiasm. She could wash them later, she had all day to wash them. She lit a cigarette and drifted through to the lounge, the 'parade room', at the front of the house, to contemplate a different expanse of rain.

Perhaps the first jolt had been the realisation that Aunt Grace did not intend to contribute any money to the project. She had given advice in plenty, and for someone who had left school at the age of thirteen Aunt Grace had remarkable business acumen, but cash, no.

For fear of losing the property the Shannons had tendered twelve hundred pounds, probably a lot more than they need have done, Aunt Grace had snorted. Then had come the news that it was only eligible for a five hundred pound grant, and though they had matched it pound for pound, depressingly little seemed to have been achieved for the money. Roofing and flooring, wiring and plumbing were essential, Laura knew, but not what she had had in mind at all.

In fact a little enthusiastic do-it-yourself on the Shannons' part would have worked wonders, but George, who in his dreams had seen himself throwing up bookshelves and room dividers with ease and skill, had proved on testing to be quite unable to knock a nail into wood or hang a sheet of wallpaper straight, and the simplest job entailed the employment of a professional.

Laura peered out of the poky little window that should have been replaced months before. To her left she could see the long stretch of Elmbridge's main street. On a bright day it was a pleasant street, very wide with a lot of attractive restored bow fronts, and big chestnut trees lining the kerb, but now rain blurred the bright paint and the delivery vans sliced up chevrons of water like snowplough blades. On her right was the narrow bridge where the heavy traffic ground to a crawl with a pneumatic wheeze, and beneath it the river, full and brown after the rain, swirling furiously around the arches of the bridge.

Laura heaved a sigh and let her gaze rove on across the bridge and along the main road out of town to where she could just distinguish the twin gables and tall chimneys of Rowan Lodge. Beautiful, desirable Rowan Lodge with its spacious sunny rooms, its safe rambling gardens bright with rowan trees, the whole lovely hillside for the children to play on. So perfectly suited to a young family, so wasted on one selfish old woman.

Laura turned away, tears of self pity gathering in her eyes. Life was such a deadly routine. Stuck in this hole every day after George had left for the office, with nothing but the chores, and the children squabbling, and shopping in Elmbridge's dowdy little shops, no Marks, no Woolies, no cinema. And George's return only meant a meal to get, and recriminations over the children's behaviour, and knitting in front of the telly after he had left for his club.

Was this all there was to life? She was only twenty-eight. She felt as trapped as if she had been locked in one of the little dark cells. If only she had a little money she could pretty herself up, a new dress, a hair-do. Laura ran a hand over the tousled blonde hair that never quite resembled the elegant upsweep she intended. They could get a baby-sitter and have a night out together, perhaps a week-end. Laura's daydreams as ever soared ahead of her.

But no, they couldn't afford it, George was always telling her. He could afford to go to his posh club almost every night, but not to take her anywhere. And did he even want to? What had he burst out at breakfast? "I don't *want* to go out every night. D'you think I want to turn out after working hard in the office all day. You drive me out with your constant whining, and the kids bawling, and this bloody house!" He had seemed near to breaking point.

They had had bad times before, why did this seem so much more drastic? Was it because such a sweet, promising dream had failed them?

But now at last she could hear the children stirring. She tensed herself and assumed her bright Dr. Spock voice. "Good morning, darlings! Aren't we sleepyheads this morning? Come along down to your breakfasts."

There was a pause, then cross muttering followed by the sound of a slap and an ear shattering yell.

Laura stiffened, clenched her fists and shut her eyes tight. Behind her closed lids she could still see Rowan Lodge, peaceful and roomy and beautiful.

"Oh, Aunt Grace," she muttered fiercely. "Why don't you die?"

CHAPTER TWO

MISS GRACE ROACH had no intention of dying. She had always been passionately interested in life, and she had just come across something that suggested a welcome break in routine. A little excitement, a scene, perhaps even tears.

As Laura muttered her imprecation Miss Roach was in her lounge at the front of Rowan Lodge. It was a very large room with long velvet curtains at the two sash windows, furnished in Edwardian fashion, with a huge sideboard, a piano, a bureau, and innumerable small whatnots. Not antiques, but handsome well-made pieces in mahogany and walnut. Dominating the room were four china cabinets housing a large collection of china, again not of great value, but tasteful well chosen pieces.

Miss Roach had been looking through the cabinets, and now she peered into them again carefully, just to be sure, before picking up a small Benares brass bell and ringing it, at the same time roaring "Annie!" at the top of a voice that could outdo any bell produced on the sub-continent.

There was a scuffling, not unlike mice in the wainscotting, and Miss Bennett appeared in the doorway, her habitual expression of apprehension well in evidence. She was a small dumpy woman, about ten years younger than Miss Roach, with a soft pale face, wispy grey hair, and desperate eyes. She stood now smoothing down her apron with nervous fingers. Miss Roach straightened her ramrod back.

"Annie, where is the fiddler?" she demanded.

Miss Bennett's mouth opened and shut foolishly.

"The—the fiddler, Miss Roach?"

"The china fiddler. The Meissen fiddler. My most valuable piece."

Miss Bennett approached her mistress and stood staring into the china cabinet as though seeking inspiration. It was a large bow-fronted mahogany cabinet with three shelves. On the bottom shelf a white and gold Rockingham dinner service was arranged, on the middle one stood half-a-dozen Staffordshire groups, while the top shelf was given over to a score of smaller figures, Dresden, Chelsea and Bow. In the centre of this top shelf stood the figure of a girl singing. She wore a sprigged gown with an apple green overskirt. There was exquisitely modelled lace at her throat and on the tiny puffed sleeves, and pink ribbons cascaded from her hair. One hand lay over her heart, the other, oustretched, held a sheet of music. Her head was flung back and the light shone almost luminously on her pearly throat and arms. She was, even at a glance, in quite a different class from anything else in the showcase. By her side was an ominous empty space.

Miss Bennett stared in horror. "He's not there," she stammered.

"I can see that. Where is he?"

Miss Bennett fluttered round the room inspecting the

other cabinets and display tables. Finally she stopped and eyed her mistress nervously.

"It's not anywhere, Miss Roach. It's gone."

"Gone? How can it have gone?"

"I—I don't know."

"You broke it, come on, Annie, own up to it."

"Oh, *no*, *no*, Miss Roach. I take great care of your pretty things."

"When did you last see it?"

Miss Bennett considered. "Last Sunday evening for certain. I wash them in rotation once a month, and it was the top shelf's turn—"

"Are you referring to last night or eight days ago?"

"Eight days ago. It was the Staffordshire's turn last night."

"And you haven't noticed the fiddler since? How about when you got the Staffordshire out and in?"

"I—I can't remember," said Miss Bennett miserably. "I think I would have noticed an empty space."

"I should hope so. Well, what can have happened to it? Do you think George or Laura pinched it when they were here yesterday?"

"Oh, no, Miss Roach." Miss Bennett was horrified. "As if they would do such a thing! You mustn't say such dreadful things!"

"All right, don't splutter. I know exactly how scrupulous my nephew is! But I expect you're right. They're born scroungers, but I don't think they'd have the guts to pinch anything. Who else has been in here?"

"No one. Nobody ever comes into the house."

"Sidney does. He waited in here when I paid him on Saturday morning. Fetch him."

"Oh, no, not Sid! It would only upset him. You know how easily upset he is. Sid would never take anything."

"He might have been attracted to it. I believe idiots are fascinated by pretty things—you know how good he is with flowers. Perhaps he took it out to have a better look at it and broke it, and then he got frightened and hid the pieces. Anyway, go and fetch him when you're told! Unless you're lying to me about breaking the figure?"

Dumbly protesting Miss Bennett hastened out of the room and through the back of the house to the garden. She hated and feared the upsets and alarms which were the breath of life to Miss Roach, and her heart pounded painfully in her breast as she scurried up and down the paths of the rambling gardens in search of Sid. She skirted the shrubbery and the kitchen garden and finally ran him to earth behind the large greenhouse.

Sid Robbins, although known as the gardener's boy, was in fact the only gardener that Rowan Lodge possessed and general handyman into the bargain.

He was a tall raw-boned man with big awkward hands and feet. He had a long melancholy face with a ruddy complexion, and vague blue eyes. There was no hint of youth in his looks or manner. He could have been any age between seventeen and thirty-five. Actually he was twenty.

He was not, as Miss Roach had implied, an idiot, but his child-like nature was geared to the slow certainties of an older, rural way of life. He was the eldest of five children of a widow who imagined no one else would have employed her dullard and was pathetically grateful to Miss Roach. Miss Roach got a docile, hardworking employee at about half the standard rate and everyone was satisfied.

Sid looked up at Miss Bennett with a wide smile. He was

very attached to Miss Bennett who he imagined stood between him and the worst of Miss Roach's wrath.

"You come for some tomatoes, Miss Bennett? I was just going to bring them up to the house."

"No, at least, not just now, Sid. Miss Roach wants to see you."

Sid put down the seed box he had been working on and looked at Miss Bennet blankly. This was a departure from routine.

"Did I do something wrong?" His voice was oddly high.

"No, no. Don't you worry, Sid. She just wants to ask you something."

They started back to the house together, the ungainly young man towering a foot over the little housekeeper. At the back door Sid cleaned his boots for a full minute. Miss Roach was waiting for them in the lounge, imperious in her leather chair.

"Come in, come in," she called. "Don't be frightened, Sid. I just want you to tell me what you did with that piece of china you broke."

This ploy was naturally quite beyond Sid's comprehension and he stared at Miss Roach blankly, his mouth open.

"Speak up, lad," urged Miss Roach.

"Was it the plant pot I broke?" Sid began cautiously. "It was an old one, it was cracked."

"No, *no*. I'm not talking about a plant pot!" Miss Roach got to her feet, took hold of Sid by the sleeve and marched him across to the china cabinet. "I'm talking about a little china figure of a man. A man playing a violin. He always stood beside the lady who is singing. He couldn't have walked away."

"No," said Sid helpfully.

"Well, did you break it?"

"Oh, no, ma'm. I never touch the cupboards. I never touch anything in the house." Sid's voice faltered. He started to back towards the door blundering into the furniture that stood in his path.

"If I thought you were lying to me—"

"I never done it. I never!"

"Of course you didn't, Sid!" Miss Bennett cried bravely. She ran to his side and glared at her mistress.

"Oh, come back here and don't be so stupid," Miss Roach growled. "I'm simply trying to find out what happened to the thing."

There was a long pause. Sid remained backed up against the wall like an animal at bay. Miss Bennett stood stiffly beside him, her face stubborn.

Suddenly Sid said, "I seen a man."

"Oh, *yes*," Miss Bennett cried. "So did I. I quite forgot."

"What? A prowler? When was this?"

"I saw him just before dinner yesterday," said Miss Bennett eagerly. "About one o'clock. You had gone into the dining-room with George and Laura and the children, and I was going down the side hall to the kitchen to start dishing up when I saw him through the window."

"Where was he?"

"He was looking over the front gate."

"Why didn't you tell me, for heaven's sake! You know the valuable things I have in my house! You know I've been attacked and left for dead once before. The police should have been fetched. The man should have been locked up!"

"I'm sorry, Miss Roach, I really am," Miss Bennett dithered. "But there was so much to do—all the dishing up, and the little kiddies' food to cut up. I did think of mentioning it after, but I knew how upset you get and I don't think the man was doing any wrong. He just looked over the gate for a minute or two and then he went off down the lane."

"With my Meissen figure!"

"Oh no, Miss Roach, I'm sure not."

"Then what was he doing up the lane, there's no other house here?"

"Perhaps he took a wrong turning."

"A likely story." Miss Roach wheeled round to Sid. "Well, when did you see him, Sid, if you're not too stupid to tell the time?"

Sid hung his head. "Be just about when Miss Bennett says." His voice was surly. "I been for a walk over the hill and I was going back home for my dinner. I watch the people coming out of church from the top of the hill, then I know if I come down slow it's just dinner time."

"Where was he when you saw him?"

"Going down our lane to the road."

"What did he look like?"

Sid turned to Miss Bennett helplessly.

"He was—just ordinary," said Miss Bennett. "Shabby, but not quite a tramp. He looked about forty. He had on a grey raincoat and a felt hat pulled down. I wasn't near enough to see his face, but he was heavily built."

"Is that the man you saw, Sid?"

Sid nodded dumbly.

"He didn't try to speak to either of you?"

He had not. Miss Roach thought for a moment, then, "Telephone the police," she said.

"Oh, no, not the *police*!" Miss Bennett squeaked. "I'm sure the man didn't get into the house. We should have heard him. And besides, Sid saw him walking away."

"Not then perhaps. He was spying out the land."

"But he didn't look the sort of person to steal a Dresden figure. Money, perhaps, or food—or a coat, but not a piece of china."

"But it has gone!" Miss Roach fixed Miss Bennett with a basilisk stare. "*Someone* is responsible. Ring the police this minute. And I only hope this new man is more competent than that fool Wainwright."

Miss Bennett crossed reluctantly to the telephone, where she stood regarding the instrument as though it was about to shoot tongues of fire at her.

"Well, what's the matter *now*?"

"You know I'm not much good with the telephone, Miss Roach. I always seem to do something wrong."

"You're not much good at anything, are you, Annie? Perhaps it's time I got somebody younger in your place."

Miss Roach hoisted herself to her feet and stomped across the lounge. In a voice that could almost have been heard in Elmbridge without the assistance of the telephone, she summoned the police.

CHAPTER THREE

EXACTLY TWELVE hours later Miss Bennett valiantly overcame her terror of the telephone and again called Sergeant Cantwell at the Elmbridge police station. Coherence would have been too much to expect, but enough of her story got through for Cantwell to immediately contact the Meddenham C.I.D. before starting out for Rowan Lodge.

Chief Detective-Inspector Matthew Furnival was on duty in his office thinking things were too quiet to last when he took the call. He noted down Cantwell's brief particulars and was checking the contents of his murder bag when Sergeant Reginald King came slowly into the room balancing a cup of coffee in each hand. He stopped and stared at the case and the coffee slopped over.

"A big one?" he asked.

"It looks more than likely, King. A place called Elmbridge. Know it?"

"Yes, it's a little market town on the edge of the Downs. About twelve miles away." Unlike Furnival, who had only recently come to Meddenham, King was a native son. "What's happened?"

Furnival took one of the cups of coffee that King still

held and gulped it. He was a big, quiet man, a little under forty, with thick fair hair and compassionate hazel eyes. "An old lady has been found dead by her housekeeper," he said. "She appears to have been smothered. Get your coat while I get on to Paston and Daly."

Daly was the police photographer, and Paston the police surgeon.

Furnival was fortunate to catch them both at home, and he left with King to pick up Daly at his house. Paston, who lived nearer Elmbridge than Meddenham, was to proceed on his own. They had stowed Daly and his gear into the back of the car and almost cleared the outer suburbs of Meddenham when King said, "What made the local man call for us? An old lady smothered—she could have turned into her pillow. It's a bit more common than murder."

"I pointed that out to him. He said there were special circumstances. He sounded as though he had his wits about him."

"Wainwright?"

"Who's Wainwright?"

"The Elmbridge sergeant. He's been there since before I joined the Force."

"This man's name is Cantwell. He sounded young and, as I said, fairly bright."

"That's right, Sarge," put in Daly. "Sergeant Wainwright retired about a year ago."

"Thank God for that," said King fervently. "I admit he was all the law Elmbridge needed ninety-per-cent of the time—he could put the fear of God into boys up apple trees, but he really was as thick as a plank. It's a good thing Elmbridge waited until this new chap came along to have its first murder, poor old Wainwright would have been having kittens."

"Well, maybe it isn't murder, but we'd better take a look."

Furnival lapsed into silence, and King and Daly into a passionate reappraisal of the Town's performance on the previous Saturday afternoon until they reached Elmbridge. There was no possibility of missing the town as the main trunk road ran straight through the middle of it. There were few lights burning in the windows and the main street was almost deserted, but one or two late dog-walkers looked round as the powerful car swept past them and across the bridge out of town. Following Cantwell's directions, Furnival turned off the main road a mile beyond the bridge into a short lane. A gate across the lane was standing open and they followed the drive, lined with rowan trees like sentinels, to stop outside a substantial Victorian villa. Doctor Paston's car was already parked on the gravelled forecourt in front of the house.

As the three detectives got out of the car, the front door of the house opened and a young man came out on to the steps. "Inspector Furnival?" he said. "I'm Sergeant Cantwell."

"I'm Furnival," Furnival said. He went up the steps to join Cantwell, a lanky young man in his late twenties, with a bright pleasant face and a mop of brilliant red hair. "This is Sergeant King," he went on, "and this is Daly." He looked up at the house. "Fair-sized place. Has there been a robbery?"

"I don't think so, sir." Cantwell led the way across the wide hall to the lounge. "I haven't had much opportunity to look around and the housekeeper is in no state to help."

He opened the door. "This is where she was found. I haven't touched anything, of course."

Furnival looked around the large room. The long velvet curtains were drawn across the windows, and he had an impression of a lot of heavy furniture and a good deal of china on display, but dominating the scene was a big leather armchair in front of an elaborate marble fireplace where a fire was just dying out. A woman was lying back in the chair. By her side a plump, bespectacled man was repacking his bag.

"It's Doctor Paston, isn't it?" Furnival said.

"Hello, Furnival. Shocking business here."

"Who is she?"

"She *was* Miss Grace Roach. She lived here alone with a housekeeper. Retired from business about ten years ago."

"Was she wealthy?"

"That was the local legend."

Furnival bent over and looked closely at the woman's body. She appeared to have been a tall, powerfully built woman for her age. She was lying in a relaxed position with a cushion behind her back. Her face was dark and congested and there was a bluish-grey tinge to her lips. Her eyes were bloodshot. Her short cropped hair was almost undisturbed. "What's the verdict, Doctor?" Furnival asked.

"Asphyxia, as far as I can tell," said Paston. "The pathologist will be able to verify it." He stood aside and Furnival saw a second large cushion lying on the floor beside the chair. "He'll want to see that," Paston added.

Furnival knelt down and examined the cushion. Half hidden beneath it he noticed a heavy walking stick. "What's the stick?" he queried. "A weapon?"

"No, she always walked with it."

"Was she feeble?"

"Good God, no. Tough as old boots."

"You knew her?"

"She was my patient. She had a touch of arthritis, but apart from that she had a remarkably sound constitution."

Furnival straightened up. He looked at the dead woman's hands. The fingers were the same bluish-grey as her features. As far as he could see with the naked eye there were no deposits under the finger-nails.

"There's no evidence of a struggle," he said. "She doesn't seem to have tried to rise from the chair. Her hair is quite tidy. What makes you think of foul play?"

"I don't think anything," Paston smiled. "Not my job, thank God."

"But you think I should get the specialists in?"

"I'll tell you one thing, she didn't turn into that pillow."

Furnival hesitated, then turned to Cantwell. "Just briefly what were these 'special circumstances' you mentioned?"

"Miss Roach called me this morning," said Cantwell. "A matter of a missing piece of china and a prowler—"

"O.K." Furnival interrupted. "Get through to Headquarters on the radio, King. Tell them to get on to the pathologist and the scientific officer. When you've finished, start checking the house for illegal entry. Daly, you can take some preliminary photographs. Cantwell, you'd better tell me the rest of what you know. We'll get out of the way while Daly does his stuff. Where have you hidden the housekeeper?"

"She's in the kitchen making tea for us, sir," said Cantwell. "She's the type that recovers quickest when she's occupied."

The two men stepped out into the hall and Furnival

selected a door. It proved to be a large dining-room. "We'll use this room," he said. They seated themselves on dining chairs and Furnival nodded at a huge carved sideboard laden with silver. "That doesn't indicate burglary."

"I don't know that it was," said Cantwell. "I haven't seen any signs of a break-in. What made me call you right away was the fact that Miss Roach had telephoned this morning. I got up here about eleven-thirty and she was in quite a state. It seems a piece of china, a figure of a man playing a violin was missing."

"Just the one piece?"

"Yes, and that's an odd thing, because it was one of a pair and everybody knows these things are a lot more valuable in pairs. There is a girl singer who goes with the fiddler."

"Where were they kept?"

"In one of the cabinets in the lounge. The cabinets are kept locked, but the keys are left in them."

"When was the figure last seen?"

"No one could positively remember seeing it since the Sunday before last, eight days ago. But Miss Bennett was in the cabinet last night and thinks she would have noticed if it wasn't there."

"I suppose the obvious solution is that Miss Bennett, or somebody, broke it and was too scared to own up."

"That seems likely," Cantwell agreed. "Miss Roach had the reputation of being a bit of a dragon. However, Miss Bennett denied it, and so did Sid Robbins. I certainly can't see him going through china cabinets."

"Who is Sid Robbins?"

"He's known as the gardener's boy. In fact he's the general factotum. He's the only other person who is around the house a lot, but he doesn't live in. He lives with his mother in Elmbridge."

"What sort of a chap is he?"

"Well, I suppose you'd call him retarded. He'd be about twenty. Big and strong, but simple-minded. I should say he's quite docile, although he was one of the ones Sergeant Wainwright warned me about."

Furnival looked up sharply. "Warned you about?"

"I'm new here, sir," Cantwell explained. "I'm not from these parts at all. So when Sergeant Wainwright was working me in he used to tell me all about the local characters and the little rackets, and who was likely to give trouble. He was a real walking encyclopaedia on Elmbridge. Not that there was very much to tell, they're a law abiding lot on the whole."

"But he did warn you about this Robbins?"

Cantwell screwed up his amiable face uncomfortably. "I don't want to give you the wrong impression, sir," he said. "Sid was just one of a score Sergeant Wainwright mentioned. It seems a few years back, when he was just coming into puberty, he took exception to some boys who were jeering at him. He went berserk and sorted them out rather decisively—put one of them in hospital for a week. But he's been as gentle as a lamb for years now, and, anyway, there was this prowler hanging around."

"When, today?"

"No, yesterday, at one o'clock. If it had been Miss Roach who saw him, I wouldn't have taken a lot of notice. That was another thing Sergeant Wainwright warned me about, Miss Roach had prowlers on the brain. She was always seeing them! But, in fact, it was Miss Bennett and Sid who had seen him."

"What action did you take?"

"There wasn't much I could do. I checked for signs of breaking and entering, there weren't any then, but both the back and front doors are open all day. Anyone could just walk in. I intended to have a word with Mr. Baer, who has an antique shop in Elmbridge, to see if anyone had tried to flog the figure to him, but he wasn't in. I asked my constable to keep an eye open for this 'prowler', but I wasn't convinced the thing had been stolen, not just one piece and so much other stuff not touched. It crossed my mind that one of the Shannon children, who had been visiting yesterday, had broken it and their parents had managed to quietly scoop up the pieces—"

Cantwell broke off at a timid knock at the door. Furnival crossed the room and opened it. On the threshold stood a small dumpy woman with a pale face and red-rimmed eyes.

"Miss Bennett?" he said.

The woman's mouth worked pitifully for a moment. "I've made some tea," she gulped, and tears started to pour down her face.

Furnival drew her gently into the room and settled her in a chair. "That's very thoughtful of you, Miss Bennett, we'll all appreciate that. Get along to the kitchen, will you, Cantwell and pass it around, and ask Sergeant King to come in here."

Cantwell left, returning in a minute with the tea. After the woman had drunk some of it and her sobs had subsided somewhat, Furnival sat down across the table from her. King came quietly into the room and seated himself in a corner, his notebook open on his knee.

"Where were you tonight, Miss Bennett?" Furnival began.

"I was visiting my sister," Miss Bennett whispered. "I go every Monday evening."

"You left Miss Roach alone?"

It was the wrong note. The tears started to flow down the woman's face again.

"I know I shouldn't have gone. I'll never forgive myself, never!"

"Now, don't upset yourself, Miss Bennett. I wasn't criticising. You have to have time off. But Miss Roach *was* alone?"

"She didn't mind. She wasn't a nervous woman."

"Sergeant Cantwell mentioned that she often imagined she saw prowlers around her premises."

"So she did. But not because she was frightened of them. She thought she was a match for any burglar. When she had her little shop many years ago a man broke in and attacked her. She'd been wanting to get her own back ever since. She just wanted them caught."

"What was the position about locking up?"

"There were Yale locks on the back and front doors, a bolt on the back door and a safety chain on the front. When I came home tonight the front door was locked, I opened it with my key, but the chain wasn't on. Miss Roach always left it off on Mondays,"—Miss Bennett's voice faltered—"when I was out."

"Were there any signs of a break in?" Furnival asked King.

"No, sir. All the windows were fastened, and the back-door was still locked and bolted."

Furnival turned back to the housekeeper. "Would Miss Roach have let a caller in at night?"

"Well—not just anybody, of course, she wasn't foolish.

But someone she knew, or a plausible stranger."

"How long were you away from the house?"

"I left at ten minutes to seven to catch the seven o'clock bus at the end of the lane. I got back at ten-thirty. I took off my coat and hat and went along to the lounge to tell Miss Roach I was back. And then—I found her."

Tears threatened to well again and Furnival pressed hastily on. "Was she usually still up at that time?"

"Yes, she went to bed at eleven o'clock."

"I presume you didn't touch Miss Roach? You left everything just as you found it?"

"Yes, sir. I could see at once that she was dead. I telephoned Mr. Cantwell because I had already met him this morning, and I told him he should ring you because of the prowler."

"Tell me what this prowler looked like?"

"I couldn't see his face, he was some way from the house and he was wearing a hat. He was a heavily built man; he looked about forty. He had on a shabby grey raincoat and a trilby with the brim turned down."

"You'd never seen him around here before?"

"No, sir."

"Has Miss Roach had any visitors lately?"

"Only the Shannons. That's Miss Roach's nephew George and his wife. They come most Sunday afternoons with their two children. They moved into the old police station in Elmbridge about six months ago when Sergeant Wainwright left. No one else ever comes."

"These Shannons—are they the next-of-kin?" put in King with his regrettably direct approach.

"I suppose they are. I've been with Miss Roach ten years and she never mentioned any other relatives."

"How did they get on with the old lady?" pursued King.

"Well—all right, I suppose. I'm sure they were very fond of her."

"And you? Did you get on all right with her?"

"Certainly I did. She was very good to me. She had her little ways, I don't deny, but she was fair and just, and she gave me a lovely home."

In return for considerable services, guessed Furnival. "How did Sid get along with Miss Roach?" he asked. "We've heard he was a bit retarded."

"That doesn't mean to say he was vicious!" the housekeeper burst out fiercely. "He was a good boy, more gentle than other lads. If Miss Roach was killed, it was nothing to do with anybody here. You'd better get off after that prowler!"

"We mean to do that, Miss Bennett. I just want you to tell me about this piece of china that is missing, and then I'll send you off to your sister for the night."

"It was the figure of a man playing a violin. It was about six inches tall. He wore a wig and striped breeches and a tan coat. Miss Roach said that it was Meissen and very valuable. It was one of a pair."

"What did Miss Roach think had happened to the figure?"

Miss Bennett bit her lip and said nothing.

"Didn't she have any idea? It's a strange thing to happen. Perhaps she accused you of breaking it?"

"No, she didn't! She knew how careful I was with her things." The woman's pale cheeks flushed. "She suggested something worse than that. It was a dreadful thing to say, and she wouldn't have said it if she hadn't been so upset."

"And what was that?"

"She—she suggested that the Shannons might have taken it."

"Was there any reason why she should have thought that?"

"Of course not! Oh, they were hard up, what with buying the house— But they would never do a thing like that." Miss Bennett's shocked protests were drowned by a considerable rumpus outside the house, as car doors were slammed, men's voices were raised, and heavy feet trampled the gravel.

"That will be the pathologist and the science boys," said Furnival. "Tell them I'll be with them in a minute, King." He got to his feet. "I think that's all for now, Miss Bennett, although I would be glad if you could go over the house as soon as you feel up to it. See if you can spot anything else missing. Now if you would get your things together, I'll see about a car to take you to Meddenham."

Miss Bennett scurried upstairs to pack a few essentials, and Furnival went outside to commandeer a car and driver from the new arrivals. When he got back to the lounge it seemed to be packed with men. King and Daly and Cantwell were there, and Doctor Macaulay the pathologist, a huge, completely bald man, who Furnival had met on several occasions. In addition there was the scientific officer from the forensic science laboratory with two of his staff. Doctor Paston had made his report to Macaulay and was preparing to leave. Furnival made his way across to the two medical men.

"How about time of death?" he asked.

Macaulay looked at him coldly, "I've been in the house exactly five minutes," he said.

"Sorry, I was really speaking to Paston."

" I'll leave it to the specialist," said Paston.

" And I'll leave it until I get her to the mortuary," said Macaulay. " Tell me what you've got so far, Furnival."

Furnival made his report. It was already past midnight and he knew it was going to be a very long night. The investigation had now rolled inexorably into its high-powered phase. He would have to work alongside the forensic scientist during his minute examination of the body and the room, he must supervise a search of the rest of the house and grounds, and then he must join the pathologist at the mortuary for the post mortem, a grisly procedure that could take many hours.

The Shannons and Sid Robbins would have to be seen first thing in the morning. Had it been daytime Furnival would have seized the chance of ducking out of the post mortem for an hour to interview them, but in the middle of the night they were not a very convincing excuse.

He had been absorbed in his tasks for half-an-hour when the telephone rang. The specialists had just transferred Miss Roach's body to a large polythene sheet on the floor, and Daly and one of the men from the forensic laboratory were busy with more photographs. Cantwell, who had been watching the specialists with great interest, answered the phone and gestured across to Furnival.

" Who is it, Cantwell?" Furnival called.

" It's Mrs. Robbins, sir, Sid's mother. She's worried about him, and she wondered if he could be here. It seems he hasn't come home, sir. He's disappeared."

CHAPTER FOUR

THE TOWN of Elmbridge had only one main shopping street to speak of, but it could boast several attractive byways that delighted visitors to the town. One of the prettiest was St. Stephen's Row, which nestled behind the church opposite the Shannons' residence. Although it was in close proximity to the busy main thoroughfare the cobbled, tree-lined street had a secluded air, and, across the old church-yard one could catch glimpses of the river swirling beneath the bridge.

In addition to the small beautiful Georgian vicarage, there were only three shops in St. Stephen's Row. The first of these was a teashop known as *Pam's Pantry* kept by a Miss Wittering. Miss *Bessie* Wittering if the truth were told, but *Bessie's Pantry* was obviously unthinkable. Miss Wittering's entire happiness lay in her teashop, which she delighted to keep pretty with fresh chintz curtains, flowers on each tiny oak table and a lot of unidentifiable brass objects hanging from the beams.

The middle of the three shops was a pet shop kept by a gentleman of great antiquity by the name of Fiddick. Mr. Fiddick's shop was something of a thorn in the flesh to Miss

Wittering. In her opinion it badly needed a coat of paint, and the large and varied stock of animals—which he never seemed to sell—were both noisy and smelly. Moreover, Mr. Fiddick talked loudly to himself and to his animals, often using shocking language.

The last shop in the row was the antique shop belonging to Bill Baer, and here Miss Wittering found it hard to criticise. It was true that Mr. Baer was a foreigner, but he had done everything in his power to overcome this misfortune. His English was almost perfect, he wore casual tweeds, and he was always ready to join in the local social life. And such a sensitive man! Miss Wittering remembered his reaction when she had popped in to tell him of the terrible news that had come down from Rowan Lodge with the milkman that morning. He had gone as white as a sheet—and Miss Roach had been no more than an acquaintance!

In his shop Bill Baer ran a duster over an exquisite rosewood table with hands that trembled slightly. Why should he feel fear at Miss Wittering's news? He had done nothing wrong, he had not seriously considered doing anything wrong. So it was not fear, but rather a sort of sick apprehension, a feeling he had thought he was over and done with long ago. He had not needed Miss Wittering to tell him that something had happened at Rowan Lodge. He was a poor sleeper, and the relays of cars going over the bridge and out along the road to the house had disturbed him. The official cars roaring through the night took him painfully back to those now dreamlike days of his early youth in the thirties. Not that the cars in the night had ever come for him. His father had been a Party member from the very beginning, he had hiked his young son miles to roar, arm extended and eyes shining, up at the new Messiah. How hard it was now to remember the passion the mad little Führer had inspired. The passion that had brought Bill Baer at the age of twenty-two floating down out of his burning plane two miles south of Elmbridge.

But not hard to remember the kindness and hospitality of the people. Baer had returned home to Berlin at the end of the war, but the shock of that hideous devastation peopled by shabby ghosts, and, worst of all, the cringing hangdog air of his once arrogant father, had sent him hurrying back to the security of the unchanging little town.

Baer walked out into the Row and shook out his duster. Glancing towards the High Street he noticed a police car waiting at the traffic lights. The driver of the car glanced casually at Baer and Baer felt himself grow colder. The man's face was pleasant, and he looked very tired, but some quality of inexorable patience sent a shudder down Baer's spine. He wondered who the man was. He knew Cantwell, the lively new sergeant, and the two local constables. He had known Wainwright well, but the only fear he could instil was for Baer's precious china as he blundered around the shop like the proverbial bull. Baer went back into his shop and tucked his duster away in a drawer. He had better not handle the china today.

Matthew Furnival sitting in his car at the traffic lights was feeling more drained than menacing. The night had been as grim as he had foreseen. He had stayed at Rowan Lodge until three a.m., when he had left with the pathologist for the post mortem at the cottage hospital. The post mortem had lasted until six a.m. and had resulted in the finding that Miss Roach had been suffocated some time between seven o'clock and ten o'clock, and that prior to that she had been a healthy woman. He had then dashed home for a wash and shave and some breakfast, and here he was at nine o'clock, back in Elmbridge, sorting out priorities for what looked like being a very busy day.

He had despatched Cantwell to see Mrs. Robbins after her phone call of the previous night, but, as soon as possible, he had to see her personally. He had instigated a search for the 'prowler', including house-to-house enquiries in Elmbridge, which he must supervise. He must go through Miss Roach's effects, see her solicitor, liaise with the forensic science laboratory, and a hundred-and-one other duties. But first he had to see her next-of-kin. He could see the old police station only fifty yards ahead of him, and, as the lights finally change and he rolled forward, an old blue Morris started up from the patch of waste ground beside the station where it had been parked, and edged into the stream of traffic. Furnival caught a glimpse of the driver, a solid fair young man, as the car passed him on its way to Meddenham. It looked as if he had just missed George Shannon.

He parked the car on the patch the Morris had vacated, and knocked on the heavy front door of the station.

Laura Shannon had been asleep when the well-informed milkman was making his rounds and was totally ignorant of the affairs of the previous night. At Furnival's knock she peered into the mirror over the kitchen sink, poked a strand of hair into place, took off her apron, and opened the door. On the steps stood a large fair man, a grave expression on his face.

"Mrs. Laura Shannon?" he enquired. "May I have a word with you? Police business."

Laura looked confused. "This isn't the police station

any more. They've moved away. It's about two hundred yards . . ."

"I know that," said Furnival. "I want to speak to you. Can we go inside?"

Laura stood to one side and Furnival stepped into the house. Through a half open door he could see a couple of small children squabbling over a littered breakfast table. Laura closed the door, snapping a warning at the children, and opened the door of the front room. The room was newly decorated and there was a lot of new and rather tasteless furniture. It was very untidy and there was a layer of dust on every surface.

"I'm sorry it's so untidy," Laura apologised. She gathered up the clutter of toys and magazines from two of the chairs and dumped them on to a third. "I haven't had time to get started yet." She perched nervously on the edge of one of the chairs. "What did you want to see me about?"

Furnival sat down. "My name is Furnival," he said. "Chief Detective-Inspector Furnival. It's about your aunt, Miss Roach."

"Aunt Grace? Why—what has happened?"

"I'm afraid she is dead, Mrs. Shannon."

Furnival's eyes searched the girl's face for reaction. Shock, relief, pleasure? A little of each, he decided. And, almost certainly, surprise.

"But we only saw her on Sunday afternoon," Laura said. "She was as right as rain then."

"I shall want to hear about your visit," Furnival said. He pulled out his notebook. "And a few other things."

"But—why? Is anything wrong? Why are you here—I mean, a detective?"

"I'm very sorry, Mrs. Shannon, but we have reason to believe that your aunt was murdered."

Murdered. The sombre word lay between them in the cluttered room, grotesquely counterpointed by the children's laughter. There was no mistaking the expression on Laura Shannon's face now. It was fear.

"She wasn't my aunt," she said surprisingly. "She was my husband's. He's not here."

"I know. I just missed him. I'll see him later, but I expect you can tell me most of what I need to know."

"When was she—killed?" Laura faltered.

"Some time yesterday evening. Miss Bennett found her when she came in at ten-thirty. Now, about Sunday. You went to lunch?"

"Yes, we go nearly every Sunday now that we live in Elmbridge. We got there about half-past-twelve and we left just before six o'clock."

"Quite a long visit."

Laura grimaced. "Too long! I mean it's a bit long for the children. They get bored and restless, and Aunt Grace has no patience with them."

"Was Miss Roach in good spirits?"

"She was never in a very good mood. Her health was all right, if that's what you mean."

"Did she talk about anything out of the ordinary? Had she had any visitors? Was she expecting a visit from anyone?"

Laura shook her head. "She didn't mention anything like that. She scarcely ever had visitors."

Furnival consulted his notebook. "Let me see, Miss Roach hadn't discovered the loss of her china figure at this time—"

"What?"

"Apparently there is a china figure missing from Miss Roach's collection."

"She didn't know about it on Sunday, or we'd have heard of nothing else all day!"

"No, she didn't discover it was missing until Monday morning, when she contacted Sergeant Cantwell."

"Well, *we* didn't have anything to do with it. Which piece was it, anyway?"

"It was a Meissen figure of a man playing a violin."

"The Meissen fiddler? That was Aunt Grace's favourite. Thank God, the kids didn't break it."

"Was it valuable?"

"Aunt Grace always said it was. It wasn't like her other stuff. She had bought that at local sales, bidding against Mr. Baer and other dealers, and everyone knew what she had paid for it. She had some nice pieces, she was supposed to have good taste—not that I care for that sort of thing myself—but nothing really valuable. The Meissen was different. There are two of them—at least there were—the violinist and a girl singer."

"The singer is still there. How did she come by them?"

"A man got them from Germany for her at the end of the war. I believe you could get anything—cameras, binoculars, fur coats—for almost nothing—"

"I remember," said Furnival. "A packet of cigarettes or a bar of chocolate. It was the currency."

"Well, this man worked in the Control Commission in Berlin. It seems he owed Aunt Grace a favour, she had been very good to his family during the Depression, keeping them going with credit from her shop. That's a bit hard to swallow if you knew Aunt Grace, but that's how she always told it. Anyway, he got this responsible job with a lot of contacts among the old aristocratic German families, and when Aunt Grace heard about the marvellous bargains that were going, she gave him some money to pick up a cut price treasure for her. He brought back the Meissen pair." Laura stopped. "Do you think the figure being missing has anything to do with her death?"

"It's hard to see how it could, nothing else seems to be missing. On the other hand it is a bit of a coincidence. Now, another matter, did you notice anyone hanging around your Aunt's house on Sunday?"

"Hanging around?"

"Yes. Anyone you didn't know."

"Oh, a *prowler*." Laura Shannon's expressive face flooded with relief. "You think she was killed by a *prowler*."

"It would seem most likely, wouldn't you say?"

"Oh, *yes*!"

"Did you notice anybody?"

"No, I can't say I did. Did Aunt Grace? She was always imagining she saw prowlers."

"She didn't see anyone. But Miss Bennett and Sid Robbins think they did. These other prowlers Miss Roach saw over the years—do you think they were genuine?"

"Well, she saw *somebody* but they usually turned out to be quite innocent people going about their business. She called Sergeant Wainwright three times in the last two years. Once it was a gypsy who probably *was* looking for what he could pick up, once it was a hiker, and the last time it was a scoutmaster mapping out a test route for his tenderfeet! She's been very suspicious ever since she was beaten up in the shop."

"It's only sensible to take precautions. Particularly women living alone in an isolated house."

"How did he get in? Aunt Grace had a chain put on the door."

"The chain was off because Miss Bennett was out. Possibly your aunt let her killer in."

"She wouldn't let a stranger in."

"Not a stranger, no."

Laura's head came up sharply. "What do you mean? You said a prowler—"

"I said someone had been seen near the house—on the previous day. There was no sign of a break-in."

There was a silence in the room during which the din from the kitchen grew too loud to be ignored. Without taking her eyes from Furnival's face, Laura Shannon backed into the hall.

"Judy! Martin! For God's sake shut up, or I'll come out and give you both a good hiding!"

She came back into the room and almost groped for her chair.

"What was the position about keys?" Furnival asked. "Who else had a key to the house?"

"No one besides Aunt Grace and Miss Bennett. She wasn't the sort to hand out keys to her house."

Furnival stood up. "I think that's about all for the moment, Mrs. Shannon. But do you mind telling me where you were last night?"

The colour drained from Laura Shannon's face. "Where I was?"

"It's just routine."

"Why—I was here. I'm always here."

"And your husband?"

"He was at his club. The Elmdale Country Club. It's on the Meddenham road."

"What time did he leave home?"

"At half-past-seven. He got home just after eleven."

"Thank you. I'll be calling to see Mr. Shannon." At the door Furnival stopped again. "Was your husband Miss Roach's heir, Mrs. Shannon?"

"I've no idea. I—we never thought about it."

Oh yeah? as King would say, thought Furnival. "Was she a wealthy woman?" he asked.

"I don't think so. She just used to keep this little shop."

"Well, never mind, I have to see her solicitor and bank manager." He smiled at her again and she escorted him to the front door.

As he descended the worn steps of the old police station he heard from the rear regions of the house a sharp slap followed by an angry wail.

CHAPTER FIVE

FURNIVAL DECIDED to leave the car where it was and do a little legwork in Elmbridge. He strolled the two hundred yards along the High Street to the new police station, noting with approval the bright shop fronts, the early English church, the ancient market hall. Elmbridge, on this crisp sunny October morning, had a prosperous and unshadowed air.

The new station was uncompromisingly modern, but its blue slate and white painted façade blended acceptably with the rest of the street. Furnival entered the vestibule and then a reception office where a young cadet greeted him with barely concealed excitement.

"Sergeant Cantwell is in his office, sir. He just came in."

Furnival knocked and entered Cantwell's office, which he noted was considerably larger and better equipped than his own. The young sergeant was seated behind his desk sorting through papers. He looked rested and alert.

"I hope you managed to get some sleep," Furnival said.

"A couple of hours, thank you, sir. Sit down. Fraser will get us some coffee. How did the post mortem go?"

"Asphyxia, just as Paston said. She was deliberately suffocated, there were signs of pressure on the mouth. It was done with that pillow that had fallen to the floor. Macaulay is going to do further tests on it today."

"When did she die?"

"Between seven and ten. No help to us at all—it's almost exactly the period Miss Bennett was out."

"If she *was* out."

"Nasty mind you've got. If, as you say, she was out."

"Could she have done it? I mean, would she have been physically capable?"

"Oh, yes. Miss Roach was ten years older and she was sitting down. Macaulay tells me that death would occur within a half to three minutes depending on the stamina of the victim. A woman of that age would probably have been dead in less than a minute." Furnival broke off as Fraser, the young cadet, entered with a tray set with coffee and biscuits.

"Good service you get," he grinned, thinking of the cooling mugs of coffee carried up two floors to his own office. He took a drink. "What about Robbins? What did his mother have to say?"

"She was very worried. He's stayed out late before, particularly when something had upset him, he likes to prowl around on his own. But he's never been out after midnight before."

"When did she last see him?"

Cantwell flipped open his notebook. "At lunchtime yesterday. He usually comes in for his dinner at one o'clock, but yesterday he got home at noon. He sat around for half-an-hour and then went out again. He's still missing, I sent Fraser to check half-an-hour ago. The mother is nearly frantic now, she's always afraid 'they' are going to 'put him away'."

"Poor devil, I don't like the sound of it. Of course, you saw him at Rowan Lodge yesterday morning?"

"Yes, sir. That was at—" Cantwell turned back a few pages of his notebook. "Miss Roach's call came through at ten to eleven. I got up there at half past. I suppose Sid took off for home as soon as I'd finished with him."

"What did he seem like then?"

"Miss Roach did most of the talking; she just allowed Miss Bennett and Sid to tell me about the prowler. What was he like? Well, I'd never spoken to him before, I don't know what he was usually like, but he seemed slightly perturbed."

"Any reports come in from the search party yet?"

"Only one. A stranger was spotted hanging around a derelict mill at Woberton, that's about five miles away. Acting suspiciously. I sent a man over, but it turned out to be a very undersized fourteen-year-old out rabbiting."

"All these things are sent to try us. I don't have a lot of confidence in this 'prowler' anyway."

"You think Miss Bennett was lying?"

"Not necessarily. But I think it's unlikely that he has any connection with the murder, and he almost certainly has no connection with the disappearance of the Meissen figure. It's not the sort of thing a prowler would lift. No, I'll still settle for an accident someone is afraid to own up to. As for the 'prowler', we'll give the appearance of concentrating on him—it will reassure the family—but I think, in fact, we should look rather nearer to home."

"If we look at the people Miss Roach would have opened the door to at night, we're looking at a very small circle,"

Cantwell said. " The Shannons, Miss Bennett, Sid, and that's about your lot."

" Yes, and it would also have to be someone who knew it was Miss Bennett's evening off."

" There is one other alternative to Miss Roach admitting him," said Cantwell. " He could have got into the house earlier in the day and hidden until Miss Bennett went out. There are plenty of empty rooms."

" Yes, that's a good point. But if it was a stranger it still leaves the question of motive."

The two men were silent for a minute, then Cantwell said, " Have you seen the Shannons?"

" Only the wife. She seems a bit—immature."

" Yes, so does he."

" You know him?"

" I see him occasionally at the country club."

" That's where he was supposed to be last night. What sort of a place is it?"

" Swanky. Expensive. And he goes there quite a lot."

" Could they be in need of cash?"

" I couldn't say. George acts like the last of the big spenders at the club, and I don't suppose he earns much of a salary. It depends whether the aunt was helping them."

" Was she rumoured to be worth much?"

" I've heard some fantastic estimates. She was the local rich, miserly recluse. There's one in every neighbourhood. But these working class fortunes are often exaggerated. I suppose the Shannons do inherit?"

" I presume so," said Furnival. " I'm seeing the solicitor this afternoon. But more important than how much she actually left them, is what they expected her to leave them."

He stood up. "I'm going to see Sid's mother now, how about coming along to smooth the way?"

Cantwell told Fraser where he could be found, and the two men walked out into the street. The autumn sunlight lit Cantwell's brilliant copper hair like a brand. After a few yards, he said, "Down here," and they turned off the main street into a narrow lane of crumbling cottages. Many of the cottages were empty, their windows boarded over, gaping holes in their roofs. Only the curtains at a few windows proclaimed that some of them were still inhabited.

Cantwell stopped before an almost paintless door near the end of the row and knocked. After a few minutes a very dirty small girl opened the door and stood staring up at them without a word.

"Is your mum in, Angela?" asked Cantwell. Almost before he had finished the question a woman scurried from the back of the house and joined the child at the door. She was a tiny emaciated woman of about forty, her lank hair and sallow skin speaking of years of poor health and neglect. Her dark eyes searched their faces anxiously.

"Oh, Mr. Cantwell, have you found him? Is he—?"

"I'm afraid there's no news at all, Mrs. Robbins," said Cantwell. "This is Mr. Furnival. Can he come in and talk to you about Sid?"

"Oh, yes, sir. Get out of the way, Angie." The woman cuffed absently at the child and ushered the two detectives into a tiny front room. "I'm that worried," she went on. "I never went to bed at all last night. I just sat at the window watching for Sid. I'm so frightened he'll get into trouble. He's a good boy, but he's simple-minded, people take advantage of him."

Furnival sat down gingerly on a filthy settee of what had

once been orange fur. White patches of damp bloomed fungus-like on the wallpaper; there was no fire in the narrow tiled grate. Worn linoleum in a pattern of big pink roses covered the floor.

"Do you have any idea where Sid might have gone?" he asked.

"He liked to go along the river—he's a wonderful fisherman. Or over the hill behind Miss Roach's house, or into the woods. He'd roam all over the place when he was in one of his funny moods."

"And he was in one of his 'funny moods' yesterday?"

"Oh, ever so! He walked in at twelve o'clock when his proper dinner-time wasn't until one, and he wouldn't say why he was early. So I fried him up a bit of bacon and put it in a sandwich. He sat at the kitchen table for half an hour and he didn't say one word, and he didn't eat his sandwich. Then off he went, still without a word."

"He took his sangwitch," muttered Angie. She seemed aggrieved on the point.

"Yes, he did, he took his sandwich," agreed Mrs. Robbins. "And that was the last I saw of him. If he doesn't come home soon he'll lose his job and Miss Roach is so good to him. Who else would have him?"

Furnival looked sharply at Cantwell.

"I didn't tell her anything," Cantwell murmured. "I didn't know whether you—"

"Quite right." Furnival turned back to the woman. "Mrs. Robbins I must tell you that Miss Roach died last night."

"Never!" Mrs. Robbins' mouth fell open in shocked dismay. "The poor soul, I am sorry to hear that. How did she die? She always seemed so robust."

"We think she was probably killed."

There was a moment's silence. Then the woman said, "Oh, God," very quietly. She dropped her head down on her knees and started to rock backwards and forwards in speechless misery. "They always said I shouldn't have kept him at home," she said at last. "But I didn't think he'd hurt anybody. He was so gentle. Now they'll lock him up for the rest of his life."

Furnival laid his hand gently on her thin shoulders. "There's nothing whatever to link Sid with Miss Roach's death—"

"People will say he did it!" Mrs. Robbins spat out fiercely. "He's different, he's mental. They'll make out he did it."

"Did what, Mam? What did our Sid do?" clamoured Angie, jumping up and down in excitement.

"Sid didn't do anything, Angie," said Furnival. "He just seems to have got himself lost and we are trying to find him." He reassured Mrs. Robbins as best he could and escaped into the street with Cantwell. "She's right, you know, Cantwell," he said. "They will say he did it. People like Sid are born scapegoats. Poor creature, she seemed to have been waiting for something like this since the day he was born."

"She's had a rough deal altogether," Cantwell said. "Sid is the oldest of five kids. The father was disabled on the railways. He finally died about six months ago."

"You know a lot about the locality, Cantwell."

"Well, you've got to, haven't you? If you're to be any good. My wife's a local girl, her family have lived here for generations. She fills me in. And, of course, Sergeant Wainwright. His records are in a horrible mess, I'm still sorting them out, but he's got it all stored away in his head."

Cantwell waited for a break in the traffic then darted across the High Street. "How about calling on Bill Baer to ask him about the figure? He's an interesting character," he went on as they safely made landfall on the other side. "He was a P.O.W. here during the war and liked it so much he couldn't wait to come back and settle down. I'm told that he's built up a very good business."

Furnival and Cantwell continued along the High Street until they reached the church where they turned into the quiet backwater of St. Stephen's Row.

Baer did not see the detectives approach. He was checking invoices in the small office at the back of his shop when the bell tinkled and stepping out into the shop he saw, silhouetted in the sunny doorway, Cantwell and the man he had noticed earlier waiting at the traffic lights.

Baer swallowed. "Good morning, Sergeant," he said. "Have you been looking for me? Miss Wittering told me you were knocking at my door yesterday."

"It was just a routine enquiry," Cantwell said. "You got off promptly—it was barely four o'clock."

"Yes, I closed a little early. There was a pre-sale viewing that I didn't want to miss over at Edendale. It's a lovely old house, I thought there might be some good stuff there."

Baer's voice had only a trace of a German accent, and the slight tremor Furnival thought he had detected when the man first spoke had smoothed itself out. He was a strikingly handsome man in his late forties with classic features, deep brown eyes, and beautifully waving silver hair. I bet the ladies love him, thought Furnival.

"Did you have any luck?" he asked.

"Luck?"

"Was there any good stuff?"

"There wasn't much in my line. The best pieces were all very large." Baer gestured round the shop. "I only have room for small pieces of furniture."

"What time did you get back?" Furnival pursued.

Baer looked at Cantwell in bewilderment.

"This is Detective Chief Inspector Furnival from Meddenham," said Cantwell. "He's helping with an enquiry."

"An enquiry? How can I help?"

"You could tell me what time you got home last night."

"I got back at seven-thirty. May I ask the purpose of your questions?"

"I'm not sure they have one. Did you know Miss Roach from Rowan Lodge?"

"Miss Wittering—my neighbour—tells me that she is dead. That she was killed last night. Is it possible?"

"It is true."

"Ach! People can no longer sleep safely in their beds. Was it burglary?"

"We don't think so. Only one thing is missing, and its disappearance was noticed much earlier in the day. That's why we have called on you. The item that seems to have disappeared is a china figure of a man playing a violin."

This time there was no doubt that Baer was rattled. His eyes grew veiled and he swallowed twice nervously before answering. "The Meissen fiddler?"

"You know it?"

"I've never seen it, but I've heard about it."

"From whom?"

"From Miss Roach. We had an acquaintance of many years. We bid against each other at sales. She liked particularly Rockingham and Coalport."

"Was the Meissen fiddler valuable?"

"I told you—I never saw it."

"But could it have been worth a lot of money?"

"An early piece, an eighteenth century piece, in perfect condition, could fetch hundreds of pounds. A really fine piece by Kandler who was the master designer at Meissen between 1730 and 1775, could fetch over a thousand. Certainly it could be valuable, but it's much more likely that it was not."

"Did you know how Miss Roach came to own it?"

"Yes. It is possible that she acquired a valuable piece in such a way. I was in Germany soon after the war ended. People were selling everything they possessed, the treasures of a lifetime, just for a meal."

"If I brought you the matching figure," said Furnival. "Could you value it for me?"

"Of course. But it is very curious that it was not taken also. A pair would be worth much more than double the value of one."

"I know that. Could there be something special about the one piece?"

"It's hard to think of anything that could be special to the one and not the other. Not if they are really a pair."

"Quite. Well, I'll see that the singer is sent down for you to have a look at, Mr. Baer." Furnival started to thread his way between the elegant little tables and desks to the door. Suddenly he turned. "Nobody has approached you with a view to disposing of the figure, I suppose?"

Baer flushed. "Mr. Furnival! I am a reputable businessman. Do you think I would do business with a murderer?"

Furnival opened the door and the bell gave its discreet

tinkle. "But I told you, Mr. Baer," he said. "I don't think the theft of the fiddler has any connection with the death of Miss Roach."

CHAPTER SIX

IT WAS five o'clock before Furnival got back to his own office at Meddenham C.I.D. After leaving Baer's shop he had eaten lunch, he had interviewed Miss Roach's bank manager, and he had kept his appointment with her solicitor.

On the way back to Meddenham he stopped at the Elmbridge Country Club. It looked, as Cantwell had described it, an expensive place, a big mock-Tudor house with manicured lawns outside and deep carpets within. Inside the revolving doors Furnival was greeted by a heavy scent of liquor, perfume and cigars. He ploughed his way through the baying laughter of the late lunchers to the bar. A young waiter produced the barman who had been on duty the previous evening, an elderly man with a sharp Irish face. Yes, the barman knew George Shannon, and yes, he had been in the club on the previous evening; what was more the man could remember exactly when. Furnival thanked him thoughtfully.

When he arrived at headquarters he was immediately whisked off to see four 'vagrants' who had been rounded up for his inspection. Of these, two could prove beyond question that they were far from Rowan Lodge at the relevant time, one was six feet four inches tall, a fact Furnival felt sure Miss Bennett would have mentioned, and the fourth would never see seventy again. He dismissed them in disgust and ran up the two flights of stairs to his office. Sergeant King was seated at his desk almost submerged beneath a mountain of reports. Superintendent Peters perched on the edge of King's desk.

"Thank God, you've come, this stuff has been pouring in all morning," said King promptly moving over to his own desk. King detested paperwork.

"What is it?" Furnival asked, taking the vacated seat.

"The usual. Reports from the lab. Reports of strangers seen in the vicinity. Any luck with that bunch they rounded up downstairs?"

Furnival yawned widely. "Not even close." He poked at the pile of reports without enthusiasm. "Aren't there any other possibles?"

"It's a bad time. There are a lot of transient potato pickers on the move. Here's one that's just come in, a farmer reports signs that someone has been sleeping in his barn. Blackett's Farm, that's near to Rowan Lodge."

"Any sign of him?"

"Not yet. Cantwell's men are combing the area."

"It's too late, he'll have moved on by now."

"Yes, well, Blackett only just happened to go to the barn this afternoon. What's been going on at your end?"

Furnival told them briefly how he had spent the day.

"So Shannon really was at this club?" said Peters when he had finished.

"Yes, but he didn't get there until nine o'clock and he left home at seven-thirty."

"How long should it have taken him?"

"Fifteen minutes at most. Of course the time lag may be nothing to do with this business. He could have been meeting a woman."

"What sort of people are the Shannons?" Peters asked.

"I only met her. She's about twenty-five. Quite pretty. Probably not much of a manager, and a bit of a whiner. I got the impression that they were marking time. The old station could be made to look quite attractive, but they don't seem to have carried anything through."

"How did they get on with Miss Roach?"

"I don't think there was much love lost. She seems to have been a mean cantankerous old creature, but who's to say you're not entitled to a little unpleasantness towards the people who are going to get the money you've worked hard for all your life."

"Are they going to get it?" asked King.

"The bulk of it, according to Mr. Dinsdale, Miss Roach's solicitor."

"Is it much?"

"It's what's known as a tidy little sum. About five thousand pounds. Miss Bennett gets a thousand and first choice of the china, Sid Robbins gets two hundred pounds, and there are a few other small bequests. The Shannons will get about three thousand, the house and the rest of the contents."

"A nice little nest egg," King commented. "But not enough to live it up in the Bahamas for the rest of their lives."

"They may well have expected more. Cantwell says Miss Roach's fortune was wildly exaggerated locally."

"Do they seem to be in need of money?"

"The bank manager had no complaints. Shannon earns fourteen hundred a year and they just about break even each month. There's a mortgage on the house, they borrowed two hundred for the car, and there's a small hire purchase on some furniture. All very typical."

"A man can get fed up with that sort of life if he's a bit of a flyer," said Peters.

"He could be a bit of a flyer if he spends as much time at that club as Cantwell says he does. It looks a bit pricey for a man in his position."

"Then how come Cantwell can afford it on a sergeant's pay?" asked King sourly.

"He married a bit of money," said Peters. "The local coal merchant's daughter. I was talking to old Wainwright about him in the spring. What did you think of him?"

"Cantwell? Absolutely first rate. Very promising. Why didn't we get him here? He's wasted in that one-horse town."

"Well, I gather he wasn't keen on settling there, he wanted to come to us, but his wife was set on moving near her parents, and, as I say, they've got the cash and they can call the tune."

"Talking of having expectations, what about Miss Bennett's thousand quid?" King enquired. "I'll bet Miss Roach was always holding it over her."

"I don't think she killed Miss Roach, not if she caught her bus according to schedule."

"Any reason? Or do you just like to think well of old ladies?" asked Peters.

Furnival smiled. "Well, I don't believe she'd have the nerve for one thing. But specifically because the curtains in the room were drawn. If Miss Bennett left the house before seven, as she said, it would still have been broad daylight."

"If she caught the bus," said King.

"We'll have to check her alibi, of course—"

Furnival broke off as a constable entered with three mugs of tea. He compared his catering arrangements unfavourably with Cantwell's. Even the Super's mug was chipped.

"It's possible that the 'prowler' and the disappearance of the figure and the murder are quite unconnected," said King.

"Quite possible, in fact even likely. The prowler could have been quite innocent as Miss Roach's previous prowlers were. What was he except a chap looking over a gate? A man doesn't make himself conspicuous where he is going to commit a murder the following day. But there *could* be connections. Sid Robbins may have broken the figure and come back in the evening, perhaps to confess. Miss Roach may have angered him or frightened him, and he killed her. Sid would have known she was alone on Monday evenings."

"Have you seen his family?" Peters asked.

"He has a widowed mother. She immediately assumed he was guilty."

"Did she, by Jove! Well, she should know what he's capable of."

"No, no, it wasn't like that." Furnival rubbed his face wearily. "She says he has always been gentle. But she's not very bright herself. She's a primitive, and when it comes to the crunch she's terrified that she *doesn't* know what he's capable of."

There was a sober pause. Then King said, "There could be other tie-ups. The prowler could have been spying out the land, later he stole the figure, and then he killed Miss Roach—"

"Why?" asked Furnival.

"He was interrupted."

"Not stealing the figure, that was missed at least nine hours earlier."

"Well—stealing something else."

"Nothing else is missing. And don't forget that Miss Roach probably opened the door to him herself, and she was still seated in her chair. That doesn't sound like a burglar."

"All right, he wasn't a burglar. Miss Bennett or Sid broke the figure. But he *was* spying out the land before killing Miss Roach for some reason unconnected with theft."

"Only Shannon has that sort of motive," put in the Superintendent.

"Well, the prowler certainly wasn't Shannon, he was inside Rowan Lodge at the time. And surely Miss Bennett would have recognised Baer—"

"*Baer*? You mean the antique dealer?" Peters was mystified. "He doesn't come into the case, does he? I thought you just went to pick his brains."

"So I did, but he seemed a bit jumpy and I found myself interrogating him."

"I hope you didn't antagonise him."

"Oh, he wasn't antagonised. He was windy. He took Miss Roach's death quite coolly, but I'll swear there was a reaction to the missing figure."

"There's probably no connection," King said. "Blokes in his line of business often sail a bit close to the wind."

"I happen to know Baer personally," said Peters stiffly. "I can vouch for his integrity in business matters."

He hoisted himself off the desk and bustled for the door.

"The inquest is at eleven o'clock tomorrow at the Shire-hall," he said. "Make sure you get there!"

By seven o'clock Furnival had sorted, and taken some action on, the essential paper work. In any case it was all the time he could spare. He went wearily down to his car and twenty minutes later was once more parking outside the old Station House.

George and Laura Shannon opened the door together, shoulder to shoulder, temporary allies. George Shannon was as blond as his wife, with wavy golden hair, pink cheeks, blue eyes, and a spoiled mouth. Although only in his late twenties he was already running to fat.

He stood aside letting Furnival into the hall. "You'll be Inspector Furnival, the wife told me you'd be coming back to see me." He smiled expansively. "You'll feel at home here, it used to be the old police station, you know." Someone had once told George that he had charm.

"Very interesting," said Furnival. "Although I haven't actually lived in a police station myself."

"It was in a bloody mess when we bought it," Shannon went on. "But we felt we ought to be near Aunt Grace. She was beginning to fail." He led the way into the room where Furnival had interrogated Laura. It was now almost unnaturally tidy.

"Children in bed?" Furnival enquired.

"Just gone up, the little monkeys," Shannon gave a false indulgent chuckle. "I expect they were making their presence known this morning, eh? I'm afraid my wife has no idea of discipline."

Furnival began to feel rather sorry for Laura Shannon. "Would you like some coffee, Mr. Furnival?" she asked, speaking for the first time.

Furnival smiled at her. "Very much. It's been one of those days."

"I expect it has," said Shannon. "Poor old Aunt Grace. I simply couldn't believe it when I heard the news. She brought me up you know."

"When did you hear?"

"Laura telephoned me as soon as you left and I came straight home. There's going to be a lot to do." Shannon did not look displeased at the prospect. "Laura was saying something about a chap hanging around the place."

"A man was seen," Furnival agreed. "But that was at Sunday lunchtime. He may have been perfectly innocent. You didn't happen to notice anyone while you were there?"

"Can't say I did. You didn't either, did you, darling?"

"No I didn't see anyone," Laura passed Furnival his coffee. "Have you caught him yet?"

"We've caught quite a selection, none of them seem to be the right man. In any case, as I say, he very likely has nothing to do with our business." Furnival turned to Shannon. "Your aunt appears to have let her killer into the house herself, so it wasn't very likely to be a stranger."

"I suppose he might have been plausible."

"But surely your aunt had already been attacked once before in her home?"

"Yes, when she had the shop. It was about ten years ago, I was away working in London at the time. It was quite a serious attack, she was in hospital for a month."

"And do you seriously suggest that a woman who has gone through an experience like that is going to open the door when she is alone at night to *anybody* she doesn't know?"

"She wasn't a nervous woman," Shannon muttered.

" Even right after the attack she was more angry than frightened—"

" No," said Furnival. " No woman in her position would have let a stranger in." He put down his empty cup. " Which leaves us with an intimate, doesn't it?"

There was a brief pause. Laura Shannon studied the new carpet, a lurid confection of green and orange flashes.

Shannon forced a laugh. " Don't tell me you think old Bennett plucked up the guts? The worm turning, eh?"

" I've been talking to the solicitor. Miss Bennet does get quite a substantial legacy," Furnival said meanly.

George's smile faded, leaving him looking quite unwell. " Really?" he said faintly.

" Yes. That's confidential, of course. But according to Miss Bennett she was out of the house before seven o'clock which is the earliest time Miss Roach could have been killed. Incidentally, speaking of times, Mrs. Shannon told me that you left the house at seven-thirty last night. The barman at the Country Club says you didn't arrive there until nine o'clock. You made a stop on the way, I presume?"

" No," Shannon said quickly. " I went straight there. You made a mistake, Laura, I didn't leave home until eight-thirty."

" No, it was seven-thirty," said Laura. " I'm sure it was. You always go out at seven-thirty."

" I don't *always* go out at any time, darling," said Shannon through gritted teeth. " I don't spend all that many evenings away from home, and I particularly remember that it was *eight*-thirty when I left the house last night."

There was an awkward silence. " I'll take the cups out," said Laura, jumping up.

When she had gone Shannon said, "What about Sid Robbins? One of your chaps said he was missing. I would have thought he was your man."

"I'm told he's unusually gentle."

"But he's mental, isn't he? He always gives me the creeps."

Furnival looked at Shannon with distaste. "We're looking for Robbins. Now what about this Meissen figure that is missing, do you have any idea what could have happened to it?"

"I expect it was broken."

"Miss Bennett denied breaking it."

"She would, if she knew what was good for her."

"Could your aunt have pretended it had been stolen, to trick the insurance company?"

"Why on earth would she do that?"

"To raise money is the usual reason. Perhaps she wanted some capital to help you get your house in order."

George gave a mirthless laugh. "You must be joking! Aunt Grace wouldn't have lifted a finger to raise money for me. Not that we wanted her money—or needed it," he added hastily.

Furnival pressed on. Shannon was expansive, but very little help. He knew of no particular enemies his aunt had had, and he had noticed no difference in her during their Sunday visit.

In the kitchen Laura filled the kettle and put it on the stove. She lit a match beneath it with trembling hands. *Eight-thirty*? No, it had been seven-thirty, she was sure. Why was she so sure? She fought to organise the thoughts that were skittering around in her head. Of course—because the children were still up. She had a distinct recollection of George swinging Martin high above his head just before he went out. He was quite good with the children, she thought bleakly, not that they really enjoyed his horseplay. They usually howled in terror, much to George's disgust. Laura brought her mind back firmly to the matter in hand. Why, why had he lied about the time? Could a man romp with a child and go straight out and—

She tried to call her mind back from that track, but it ignored her. She felt as though the safe sure earth had flown out from beneath her feet and she was plunging into a horrifying abyss. An abyss where George was no longer the familiar figure she had known for so many years, but a blurred photograph in a lurid Sunday newspaper. Her errant mind began to visualise the black headlines; she was not far from hysteria now, her knees and hands shook, and a scream was welling in her throat, a piercing scream that deafened her, and went on and on and would not stop. . . .

Suddenly Furnival appeared in the kitchen doorway. He looked at her face and walked over and removed the screeching kettle from the flame. Then he took her firmly by the arm and put her in a chair.

"It *was* seven-thirty, wasn't it, Mrs. Shannon?" he said.

"Where is George?" Laura asked quickly.

"He's in the lounge. I told him I wanted a word alone with you."

"It was eight-thirty," Laura said. "I remember now. I made a mistake this morning."

He could not shake her. George joined them in the kitchen and there was no further opportunity to work on Laura. All the same, Furnival was sure that her first version of the time had been the right one and Shannon had had an hour to kill somewhere. He left the house soon after. It was nearly nine o'clock and he was out on his feet. He called in at Cantwell's office to find out whether anything important had come in. It had not, and there was still no word on Robbins or the mystery prowler.

CHAPTER SEVEN

FURNIVAL SLEPT until six the following morning, then breakfasted and drove back to Elmbridge. Cantwell had not yet got in to work, but two members of the murder squad were keeping an eye on three vagrants who had been picked up earlier that morning sleeping rough. Furnival sent one of them packing, and made arrangements for Miss Bennett to see the two who were not too unlike her description. Then he returned to Meddenham and put in an hour in his office before leaving for the inquest.

There were no more than a dozen people gathered in the small room at the back of the Shirehall, and most of those were officials. The proceedings were informal and very brief. George Shannon, in a black armband, gave evidence of identity, Macaulay, the pathologist, described the cause of death, and Furnival reported that enquiries were being pursued. The coroner then issued the burial order and adjourned the inquest.

Furnival was back in his office within an hour. Superintendent Peters was again waiting for him.

"How did the inquest go?" he asked.

"The usual. Adjourned."

"Hm. What about the Yard, Furnival, do you think we should call them in?"

"I'd like another twenty-four hours."

"Well, I'll put it to the Chief Constable, but you know how peeved they get if we wait until everything is stone cold. Is there any progress I can report?"

"We've got two vagrants in custody at Elmbridge. I'm going to get Miss Bennett to look at them."

"Do you think one of them might be our man?"

"Frankly, no, I don't, sir."

"What did Shannon have to say about his delay in reaching his club?"

"He said he didn't leave home until eight-thirty on Monday evening. His wife backed him up, but I'm inclined to believe her first story."

"Put a bit of pressure on him. Could he be a killer? Has he got it in him?"

Furnival gave it some thought. "Well, they're neither of them very likeable people, but I don't think they are 'doers'. I think they go with the tide. Things happen to them."

"I know what you mean. Did he give you any help at all?"

"No. He'd like to lumber Sid Robbins with the deed."

"He could be right, you know. Is there any sign of Robbins?"

"Not yet, sir."

"We've got to find him," said Peters grimly. "Anybody like that on the run gets the public very jumpy. You'd better get back there on the spot, Furnival. I can't give you much longer before calling in the Yard."

It was half-past-twelve. Furnival left directions where he could be found and went down to the canteen in the basement where he found Sergeant King. They grabbed a quick lunch together before setting out for Elmbridge once more. The road was beginning to look very familiar.

"What did the Super have to say?" King asked.

"He's started making noises about the Yard."

"I expect the Chief Constable is breathing down his neck."

"Yes, I know, and we haven't much to work on. I want to have another word with Baer. Cantwell had the remaining Meissen figure taken down to him—he should have had time to examine it by now. Then I'm going out on the hunt for Sid Robbins. I feel that's the vital operation."

"I agree," said King soberly. "I hear the good people of Elmbridge have tried and convicted the poor bastard already. They're fit to lynch him on sight."

At the Elmbridge police station they found Miss Bennett drinking a cup of tea while she waited for the proceedings to begin. She looked ill and tired in her cheap grey coat and cotton gloves. Furnival hoped she would have a bit of fun with her thousand quid. He explained carefully to her what she was to do and, with Cantwell, escorted her to a passage at the rear of the station where the two men had been lined up for her inspection. One was a scruffy, brutal-looking fellow in a long army surplus greatcoat. The second was more of a possibility. He was reasonably clean and decent and he wore a grey raincoat.

Miss Bennett crept nervously forward, stole a furtive glance at each of the men, and scurried back to the detectives.

"No," she whispered.

" Are you quite sure?" asked Furnival. " Don't be afraid to take a good look."

Miss Bennett shot another quick glance. " I'm positive, they're nothing like the man."

" All right, thank you. Fraser will see that there's a car to take you back to Meddenham."

Furnival and King went out into the High Street. It was early closing day, and the road was much less busy than usual. Elmbridge, on the bright October afternoon, displayed some of its lost small town charm. In St. Stephen's Row only a couple of late lunchers lingered in *Pam's Pantry*. The pet shop and Baer's shop were closed.

Furnival rattled Baer's door gently, and after a moment he emerged from his office. He shot a couple of hefty bolts on the door and let the two detectives into the shop. He relocked the door and led the way back to his office.

The office was tiny and cluttered; on two sides of it glass partitions overlooked the shop. The floor space was almost filled by a large oak desk with a swivel chair behind it, but in addition several small pieces of furniture in the process of being repaired stood against the walls. On an elaborate Adam mantelpiece stood an assortment of broken porcelain figures. There was a large gilded convex mirror hanging on one wall.

Baer found a couple of chairs for Furnival and King, upending one that had been lying on the floor and wobbling it gingerly. " There you are, gentlemen, I think it will now hold you."

Furnival looked around. " You do your own repair work?"

" Yes. I taught myself. In fact, other dealers now send me china to repair." Baer opened the top drawer of his desk and took out a china figure. He cleared a space on the littered surface and set it down. "Well, there she is."

Furnival looked at the Meissen singer. She was about six inches high, dressed in an apple green and flowered dress. There was lace at her bosom and sleeves, and ribbons cascaded from her hair. One beautifully modelled hand lay over her heart, the other, outstretched, held a sheet of music. Her head was flung back and her rosy lips were parted. She was frozen forever in the delight of her song.

"It's beautiful," said Furnival. He picked the figure up gently in his big hands. "Absolutely beautiful."

"Yes," agreed Baer. "She is."

"How much is it worth?" asked King.

"If the fellow was in perfect condition like this, I would have given Miss Roach fifty pounds for them."

"Fifty pounds! Is that all?"

"I'm afraid so. It is not an early piece, it is late Victorian."

"But—it's so perfect."

"Of course, that was their secret, perfection. They could do it again and again."

King took the figure from Furnival and looked at it reverently. "How can you be so sure?" he asked.

"Oh, many things. Glaze, modelling, colours. I'm afraid there is no doubt."

"It's exquisite," King said.

"But not rare. Dresden, as we should call it, was a factory with a long age and a huge output. Beauty is not relevant. It is the idiotic economics of supply and demand."

Baer seemed altogether more at ease in his professional capacity.

"It is not so much what a thing is worth," he went on,

"as what someone may have thought it was worth."

Furnival looked at him. "Quite. I suppose Miss Roach's Meissen figures could have been almost as much a local legend as her fortune." He stood up. "Thanks very much for your help, Mr. Baer. I'll see that the figure is taken back to the house."

Baer let them out into the Row. They passed Mr. Fiddick's fly-blown windows. Outside *Pam's Pantry* Furnival halted.

"Feel like a cuppa, King? I caught this lady's eye yesterday. I think she may like to chat."

Miss Wittering was thrown into quite a flutter by their entrance. She was glad that she was wearing the forget-me-not blue smock that matched her eyes, and made her resemble, she imagined, one of Mr. Baer's Dresden shepherdesses. She hurried forward and led Furnival and King to a small round table, flicking a duster over its dazzling surface.

"A pot of tea, please," said Furnival.

"And some cakes?"

"It's a little early."

"Oh, you *must* try my cakes. Everything is home-made, and although I say it myself, I do have the touch!"

"I expect I could manage a couple," said King, who could eat at any time.

Miss Wittering tripped happily away to the quarters where she worked her magic and King turned to Furnival. "Did Baer mean that Shannon may have thought the figure was very valuable?" he asked.

"Somebody may have—it didn't need to be Shannon. I would have taken it to be valuable myself."

"Maybe Baer was driven mad by never getting a peep

at this legendary Meissen, broken into Rowan Lodge to see it and smashed it in his nervousness. You said he acted guilty when you first mentioned it."

"A bit far fetched. Baer is a dealer, not a fanatic collector. And he is probably far less likely to drop china than most people!"

Miss Wittering returned and started to set the table.

"Did you find Mr. Baer at home?" she enquired. "I noticed you at his door."

"Thank you, yes. He was most helpful," Furnival responded.

"Oh." Miss Wittering's eyes widened. Furnival saw, 'Man helping police with enquiries', telegraphing across her mind, and cursed the popular press. "A professional matter," he went on. "He gave us his opinion on a piece of china."

Miss Wittering looked unconvinced. She departed to return a minute later with the teapot, a plate of cakes, and a plate of buttered scones. The two men drank their tea, King tucking into the cakes with such enthusiasm that Furnival was induced to join him. When Miss Wittering returned twenty minutes later the plates looked as though they had stood in the path of locusts.

"My you have made a good tea!" she cried delightedly.

"Very nice indeed," said King, leaning back in his chair and rocking the little table alarmingly on his knees.

"I'm so glad it found favour," Miss Wittering breathed. She wrote out their bill, a transaction she never enjoyed. She preferred to think of her customers as guests.

"I expect you know we're police officers," said Furnival. "We've been making enquiries about any strangers who may have been seen around the town. One in particular, a shabby, heavily-built man of about forty wearing a grey raincoat. He was seen near Rowan Lodge at lunchtime on Sunday."

"I haven't noticed anybody like that." Miss Wittering was almost pop-eyed with excitement. "I don't open on Sundays, of course."

"He didn't come in here on Monday or yesterday? Would you have remembered him?"

"Good gracious, I don't have that class of person in here!" Miss Wittering cried. She shuddered delicately. "Poor Miss Roach. What a dreadful thing to happen! But she was very foolish to keep all that money and her priceless antiques in that lonely house."

"Common gossip, was it, that she kept wealth in the house?" Furnival suggested.

"Everybody knew it. And they knew that Miss Bennett visited her sister every Monday night leaving Miss Roach alone in the house. It's very silly to be so regular, criminals get to know your routine, you know. When she wasn't on the bus as usual on Monday night I thought Miss Roach must be getting a bit more careful at last—"

"Miss Bennett wasn't on the bus?" broke in Furnival. "The seven p.m. to Meddenham?"

"That's right," said Miss Wittering. She saw she had hit the jackpot this time and warmed to her theme. "Miss Bennett travelled on that bus every Monday night as long as I can remember. I go to a whist drive in Meddenham most Monday nights, so I suppose I'm regular, too, but my little treasures wouldn't interest a burglar! Anyway, last Monday I said to the bus driver—Tom, it was—'Where is Miss Bennett tonight? Have you left her behind?' And he said he had waited a couple of minutes at the bottom of her lane and even given a toot, but she hadn't come. Tom knows his regulars, you see."

Furnival paid the bill and the two men left the café.

"We'd better see the sister," King said soberly.

"I noticed some buses standing in the square near the market hall," Furnival said. "We'll try there first. If we can find Tom we'll have verification."

The market hall was almost opposite the police station. In the cobbled square behind it three buses waited, one with its engine running. Small queues of people formed at different points. It was some kind of terminus. Furnival decided that Tom, who knew all his regulars, would be a solid type. He made his choice and approached a burly bald-headed driver who was leaning against his radiator smoking half-an-inch of cigarette.

"I'm looking for a driver by the name of Tom who drove the seven p.m. bus from Elmbridge to Meddenham on Monday evening," Furnival began.

"Why?" asked the man, instantly suspicious.

"A routine police enquiry. We're not the traffic control, there's no need to worry."

"Why should I worry? If everybody was as careful as me . . . I'm Tom Forrester, and I did that run. What do you want to know?"

"I believe you usually pick up an elderly lady at the bottom of the drive to Rowan Lodge? It's a big house about a mile before you get into Elmbridge."

"I know where it is. Usually? Always, is more like it. I could set my watch by her."

"How about last Monday?"

"She wasn't on last Monday."

"Are you sure?"

"Sure I'm sure. I waited a minute for her. I got to get going now. I'm late out."

The driver opened his cab door and swung himself up into the seat.

"Just a minute," said Furnival. "Who drove the bus after yours on Monday?"

Forrester thought for a moment. "The eight o'clock? That would be Len Carver. Over there on the 917."

"Thank you," said Furnival. With King he sprinted over to a bus on the far side of the square. This driver sat in the driving seat reading a lurid American comic. He was very young, no more than twenty, with a pimply face and lank hair. As Furnival feared, he remembered no one from his Monday run, or only, when further pressed to put his inadequate mind to work, a smashing blonde the shortness of whose skirt you wouldn't believe.

Furnival and King walked slowly from the square to their parked car. "Why are people such bloody liars!" Furnival exploded. "First Shannon, now Miss Bennett. We'll have to go back to Meddenham and see her, just when I wanted to be on the spot in case Robbins turned up."

CHAPTER EIGHT

AT JUST the same time as the exasperated Furnival was leaving Elmbridge, Betty Booth stopped her Mini outside the vacant semi in Oakfield Avenue on the outskirts of Meddenham. Her face fell slightly as she took in the faded paint and mean proportions of the place. She had only been house-hunting for a short time and she had not yet learned to distrust the house agents glowing phrases. 'Attractive modern semi-detached in superior residential area. Gardens back and front.' Betty looked doubtfully at the 'front garden'; a bare six feet in depth. 'Timber garage'—that would be the rotting hulk she could see lurking among the waist high grass at the back. Still, it was within their price range, and Derek was wonderful with his hands.

She got out of the car and, lifting the sagging gate to one side, walked up to the front door. The filmy cobwebs around the door showed that no one had even looked at the house for a long time. Perhaps they could get it for a really low offer.

She stepped into the tiny hall and a musty depressing smell hit her. She propped the front door open to let in some fresh air, and opened the door to the 'lounge'. Her heart sank. It was so *small.* The lovely three-piece suite Mum and Dad had given them would barely go in, let alone the telly. And that dreadful little grate with the pea-green tiles—how had people lived in such houses? Betty went on into the 'compact dining-room' at the back. The room was extremely dark but she could plainly see the chalky white patches of damp on the walls. In fact the whole house smelt damp, with an icy chill that entered her bones. She hurried into the tiny kitchen and stopped in horror. So *that* was a 'glazed sink'! Rotting floorboards, a minute window, banks of unconcealed pipes and meters, it simply would not do at any price. Betty made for the front door; at the foot of the stairs she paused. She could just have a peep at the bedrooms, to tell Derek she had seen the place properly. At least it looked a bit brighter up there.

She climbed the staircase, wondering why she was tiptoeing, and pushed open the nearest door. It was a tiny bedroom at the back of the house. Betty smiled sentimentally at the faded nursery wallpaper. We must have three bedrooms, Derek had said, so that it will be big enough for later. She blushed rosily as she gazed at the yellowed figures of Mickey and Donald and Pluto. Perhaps the paper had been there since the house was built. Where was the baby now, she wondered, who had lain gurgling up at these bright images; and felt sorry for despising the house. She crossed to the window to look over the back garden. And from the front bedroom she heard a tiny stifled cough.

Betty's heart gave a lurch and her knees almost buckled beneath her. For a moment she thought of ghosts. Had she, dreaming of that long ago baby, somehow peopled the house? She felt the skin crawl on her scalp. Then there was another slight sound, the shifting in position of an unmistakeably human body. Betty stood rooted to the spot, clutching her handbag, the keys, the house agent's letter, in stiff fingers. I must move, she thought, or make some casual sound, cough—or whistle—so that he will think I didn't hear him. But no, she realised with despairing certainty, it was too late. He knows I have heard him. But still she stood rock still, her mind racing. Can I make it to the stairs? Should I break the window and scream? Where *is* he? Then suddenly there was a loud, no longer furtive, noise of a large body lumbering to its feet. It broke the spell. Betty whirled across the room, through the door, and swung round the bannister post. As she did so a man burst from the front bedroom, a big man wearing a grey raincoat and a slouch hat, and with a look of desperation on his face.

He rushed along the landing, the rickety floorboards trembling beneath his feet. He grabbed Betty's wrist, shouting something at her. Betty twisted her hand in the man's agonising grip. She felt her feet shoot from under her as she went sliding down the staircase, with the man stumbling and crashing on top of her. He still gripped her arm, shaking her, and shouting at her with his terrible face close to hers. A helpless faintness enveloped her, but just before she blacked out she heard herself screaming again and again.

Half a mile away, Furnival and King were ascending to the fifth floor council flat of Mrs. Alice Milton, Miss Bennett's sister. They located the door and their ring was answered promptly by a small plump woman who, although ten years younger and carefully permed, still bore an unmistakeable resemblance to her sister.

"Is Miss Bennett at home?" Furnival asked.

"Shh!" The lady hushed them fiercely, glanced up and down the passage, and almost pulled them inside the flat.

"Thank goodness, you're not in uniform," she breathed. "Although any fool could tell you're from the police. No, Annie isn't at home. She's gone for a walk."

"May we wait?"

"I suppose so. You'd better come in." She grudgingly opened the door of the living-room and Furnival and King entered. It was a small room, very brightly furnished and over warm from a fire of electric yule logs that twinkled in the hearth. The floral curtains and covers and the multi-coloured cushions had a somewhat dazzling effect, but it could have seemed like home to Miss Bennett. From the kitchen came the smell of a fish tea.

"Sit down," ordered Mrs. Milton. "I've got to go and turn the kippers."

"Would you come back for a minute after," said Furnival. "I'd like a word with you."

Mrs. Milton stomped out, and Furnival and King were left contemplating the innumerable gew-gaws that crowded the room. Souvenirs cast in every form that man's ingenuity could devise covered every available surface—drunks embracing lamp-posts, small girls losing knickers, nodding dogs, furry 'gonks', tiny useless brass items, and cream jugs with lugubrious proverbs in pseudo Devonshire dialect.

Furnival's bemused gaze reeled back from a two feet tall plaster statue of an inadequately draped young woman who was having difficulty restraining an Afghan hound. He looked at his watch. "I hope Mrs. Milton can leave her kippers to fend for themselves. I want to talk to her before Miss Bennett gets back."

At that moment Mrs. Milton returned from the kitchen, and sat down across the hearth from them.

"It must be very pleasant for Miss Bennett to have this place to come to," Furnival said.

Mrs. Milton thawed in an instant. "It's always been a second home to her," she said. "I told my Frank when we married, 'My home is Annie's home!' Well, it was obvious by then she was never going to get a man of her own. She was thirty-five and never much to look at. So wherever she worked she got here as often as she could, and since she's been so near at hand with Miss Roach it's been once a week without fail. Every Monday night."

"And this Monday night?"

"Of course. Didn't she tell you?"

"Yes, she did. But, you understand, in a murder investigation we have to check every statement."

"You needn't doubt my sister's word. We come from a respectable family."

"I'm sure you do, Mrs. Milton. So last Monday was just the same as usual?"

"Yes. Apart from Annie being an hour late."

"She was an hour late?"

"She arrived at half-past-eight instead of half-past-seven. I was beginning to worry a bit, she's so regular."

"Did she give any reason for changing her routine?"

Mrs. Milton looked embarrassed. "I really shouldn't tell you. Annie would be cross. But the truth of it is she'd had a little tiff with Miss Roach, or, more likely, Miss Roach had been bullying her again, Annie has no spirit to stand up for herself. When she was due to leave for her bus she reckoned people would see that she'd been crying, particularly that nosy old Miss Wittering, so she stayed in her room with cold pads on her eyes until she looked more presentable. By that time her bus had gone and she had to wait an hour for the next."

"I quite understand," Furnival said. "Did your sister give any explanation for Miss Roach's bad temper?"

Mrs. Milton laughed shortly. "That old dragon was always in a bad temper. I think Annie said she accused her of breaking an ornament while she was dusting. Of course Annie was a companion, I wouldn't like you to think she was in service or anything, but she did light chores to oblige."

"Quite. And had she broken the ornament?"

"If she said she hadn't, she hadn't. She's always most careful with my little treasures. And I don't think I should answer any more questions. I'm sure Annie has told you all this herself." Mrs. Milton jumped from her chair and stretched to her full five feet.

Furnival and King got to their feet, not sure whether they were being evicted. Furnival was about to make some attempt at pacification when they heard footsteps outside in the hall. The door opened and Miss Bennett stood on the threshold, still in the drab grey coat she had worn that morning. For a moment a look of fear slid across her face, then she recovered herself.

"Good afternoon, Mr. Furnival. Have you got some more men for me to see?"

"Not yet, Miss Bennett. But I expect we'll have to bother you again."

"It's no bother. I'd like to be of help." Miss Bennett removed her coat and gloves, and sat down on the edge of a chair.

"You didn't attend the inquest?"

"I wasn't called."

"No, but I thought you might be interested."

"No." Miss Bennett closed her lips stubbornly. "I didn't want to go. Lawyers try to mix you up. They twist what you say."

"You wouldn't have been required to say anything," said Furnival.

"Anyway, why not?" put in King. He lit a cigarette, and drew towards him an ashtray in the form of a lop-eared doggie chewing a bedroom slipper. "Why not give evidence? You didn't tell us any fibs, did you, Miss Bennett?"

The woman's face went red and then very pale.

"No," she whispered. "Of course I didn't."

"You just forgot that you didn't catch the seven o'clock bus that night? It slipped your mind that you were in the house until nearly eight o'clock? Well into the period when Miss Roach was murdered."

There was a moment's complete silence, then a sort of eldritch screech from Mrs. Milton. "How dare you speak to her like that! It's police persecution, that's what it is."

"Now, now, Mrs. Milton," Furnival managed to intercede. "Sergeant King didn't intend to upset you. But the fact remains that Miss Bennett made a false statement that has involved us in considerable extra work. You do understand that we have to double check false statements in a case of murder?"

"Well, it was silly of her," muttered Mrs. Milton, partly mollified. "But I explained about the bus. Good gracious, look at her? Does she look as though she could harm a fly?"

The two detectives looked at Miss Bennett. A plain, shabby, brow-beaten elderly woman, even now the tears were starting to well again in her red-rimmed eyes. As

George Shannon had asked, could the worm have turned?

"What about the bus, Miss Bennett?" Furnival asked. "Will you tell us now what really happened?"

Miss Bennett pressed a handkerchief to her eyes and sniffled a little. "Miss Roach was so horrid to me," she whispered. "She said such unkind things. I was afraid—under the circumstances—to tell you. She made me cry and I looked such a sight I couldn't face going on the bus. So I bathed my eyes and put on a little powder, and then I went out at a quarter-to-eight to catch the later bus."

"Does the rest of your statement still stand? No one came to the door? You didn't see anyone?"

"Oh, no!"

"Well, are you satisfied?" Mrs. Milton demanded tartly. She held the door open for Furnival and King. "If there's nothing else you want to pester us with, Mr. Milton's kipper will be spoiling!"

"*Are* we satisfied, King?" asked Furnival. They had just arrived back in his office from the redoubtable Mrs. Milton's eyrie.

"Not by any means," said King firmly. "Murder by lady companion is not unusual, particularly when they're mentioned in the will! And the method, smothering with a pillow, is just the sort of caper they think up. Anyway—missing her bus for the first time in years!"

"I should have thought it was the one time she would have made very sure of catching her bus. Doing everything as usual, in fact."

"You think it was just a coincidence?"

"Not exactly. Missing the bus sprang out of the events of the day, and Monday does not seem to have been a very usual day at Rowan Lodge. The undeniable thing that emerges from Miss Bennett's new statement is that it shortens the time Miss Roach was alone in the house by an hour. She could only have been killed between *eight* o'clock and ten o'clock."

"Unless," said King. "She was killed by Miss Bennett."

He broke off as the telephone on Furnival's desk shrilled. It was the internal line from Superintendent Peter's office.

"Oh, you're back, are you, Furnival?" he began to gabble as soon as Furnival lifted the receiver. "Where the hell have you been? I've been ringing all over the place for you."

"I'm sorry, sir. I've been with Miss Bennett, the housekeeper. There was what could have been a serious discrepancy in her statement. She gave quite a reasonable explanation, but I don't know—"

"Never mind that now. it probably doesn't matter any longer. Get down here right away. We've got your man for you. The vagrant. He was picked up here in Meddenham over an hour ago. He attacked a young woman."

CHAPTER NINE

FURNIVAL AND King took the stairs to Peter's office at the double. The Superintendent was waiting for them in the corridor outside his door with Kennedy the station officer.

" I'm sorry I couldn't be found," Furnival said again.

" It hasn't done any harm," said Kennedy. " He's stewing nicely." Kennedy was a grey-haired man with a deceptively sweet expression nearing retirement age. Hardened criminals had been known to weep on his fatherly shoulder before they discovered their mistake. " He's ready to make a statement," he added.

Furnival stared. " A confession?"

" You're joking. He's innocent, of course. White as driven snow. Aren't they all?"

" Is it anybody we know?"

" No. He's got no record here," said Kennedy. " We've contacted the Criminal Record Office to see if they've got anything. His name is Murphy. Kevin Murphy."

" What about the girl he attacked?" Furnival asked.

" She's not much hurt," said Peters. " More frightened than anything else."

" What happened?"

" He had taken refuge in an empty house, and young

Mrs. Booth arrived with an order to view from the house agent. She stumbled on him, and he tried to prevent her leaving. Fortunately her screams reached a couple of chaps working in the garage of the house next door. If they hadn't heard her it might have been much more serious. As it was they managed to overcome Murphy and a passer-by rang for us."

As Peters was speaking the four men made their way down the corridor to the charge room. Kennedy flung open the charge room door. A man was seated on one of the wooden chairs in the nearly bare room, an empty tea cup on the table in front of him.

"This is Chief-Inspector Furnival," Kennedy announced to the man. "He's in charge on this case. Keep a civil tongue in your head and don't go telling him no lies!"

Murphy raised his head. His hair was dark and matted, and his skin was weathered. He was unkempt, but not filthy and his features were not unpleasant.

"Good evening, Murphy," said Furnival. "Had your tea?"

"Yes, sir, thank you, sir." The man put both his hands on the table and half stood up. "I'm sorry about the young lady. I never meant to hurt her. She got frightened. I only meant to stop her."

"Stop her! Half kill her, you mean," snapped Kennedy.

"All right, Sergeant, I'll take over," said Furnival. He exchanged a few words with the Superintendent, who left with Kennedy. Furnival and King sat down at the table with Murphy. Sergeant King took out his cigarettes and offered them to Murphy who took one eagerly.

"Want to make a statement, do you?" asked Furnival. "You know you are not obliged to say anything unless you wish to do so, but what you say may be put into writing and given in evidence? Now, do you want to write it yourself, or shall Sergeant King take it down? You can read it through and correct anything you want to before you sign it."

"The sergeant can write it down, I'm not much of a hand at writing, but I'm glad to be talking to you. I never done nothing, that's God's truth."

"Why were you hiding in that house?" asked Furnival.

"I saw in a newspaper how that old lady was killed and you were looking for a man."

"What made you reckon you were the man?"

Murphy said nothing.

"Was it because you'd been hanging around Rowan Lodge?" Furnival pressed.

"On Sunday morning I was. I admit it. I wasn't doing anything wrong."

"What *were* you doing?" put in King.

"I was looking for work."

"Work!" King's tone was scoffing. "I'll wager that's one thing you never look for. What were you trying to knock off?"

"I wasn't trying to pinch anything. I'm a working man, I've got me cards to show." His eyes swivelled desperately to Furnival. "Straight up, sir, I've never been in trouble with the police."

"Where were you last in regular work?" asked Furnival.

"On a building site down Bristol. They wanted me to work high, but I don't like going up high, I get dizzy spells, so I packed it in."

"When was this?"

"In April, sir."

"That's six months ago. What have you been doing since then?"

"Bit of this and a bit of that. I can turn me hand to anything. I had a week putting up tents for the agricultural show. Then I took to the country for the fruit picking and stayed out for the spuds. I thought the country air might do me good. I got a bit of a chest."

"I shouldn't imagine sleeping rough in October would do it much good. Do you usually sleep out?"

"No, sir, and I never thought I'd come down to that, but the money was running a bit low."

"Do you have an address?"

"Not a home as you might say. But there's a couple of lodging houses in Meddenham where they know me and should speak well of me, for I've never been a bit of trouble to them." Murphy extracted a grimy handkerchief and mopped his face with it.

"O.K.," said Furnival. "Let's start with last Sunday when you were innocently hanging around Rowan Lodge. What time would it be?"

"I couldn't say exactly. Getting on for dinner time. I was thinking maybe I could do some odd jobs for a bit of grub, when I saw this woman looking out at me. She didn't look very friendly, so I decided to try my luck somewhere else."

"How did you come to be near the house? It's off the road." Furnival resumed.

"I'd been kipping in a barn nearby, about two hundred yards down the road—"

"That would be Blackett's barn, the one Cantwell's men turned over," King interrupted.

"When did you sleep in the barn?" Furnival asked.

"Saturday, Sunday, and Monday nights. I'd been working at Blackett's farm over the hill the previous week, picking potatoes. I slept in a lodging house in Meddenham during the week, but, what with bus fare and doss money, my cash was running low. Then I spotted this barn, and it was dry and warm and handy."

"Blackett doesn't hire pickers on a Sunday," Murphy went on, "so I slept until about eleven, then I thought I'd have a stroll around. I was hoping for a meal, or at least a cuppa, at the house with the rowan trees, but there was nothing doing, so I walked out along the trunk road to a transport café, the *Black Cat*. It's about four miles from Elmbridge. I had my dinner there. At night I went to a pub, the *Foster Arms*, I think it's called. I stayed there till closing time. I didn't have a lot to drink. I can make them last. Then I went on to the barn and slept for the night."

Furnival looked across at King who nodded. "There is a pub of that name, it would be about a mile past Rowan Lodge."

"O.K., Murphy," Furnival said. "Now what about Monday."

"I had a bit of a shock on Monday," Murphy replied. "I didn't get taken on at Blackett's. He'd more or less promised another couple of days, it was all I'd hung on in the neighbourhood for, but when I got there he'd got a field full of school kids picking. Taking the food out of working men's mouths! Just because he can get them for a few bob cheaper!"

"What did you do?"

"I tried a couple of other farms, but there was nothing doing. The rest of the day I spent much the same as Sunday.

I walked out to the *Black Cat* for my dinner, and I went to the *Foster Arms* at night."

"Exact times, please, for Monday. It's important."

"I don't have any idea of the times!" burst out Murphy. "Why should I? I'd got nothing else to do but wear out my shoe leather tramping up and down that bloody road!"

"Well, think about it. When you got to the pub was it still daylight?" asked Furnival.

"It was just dusk as I got there."

"That makes it about eight o'clock. Did you stay until closing time again?"

"No, I could only afford a pint. I made it last as long as I could, but—"

"But not until closing time," said King sadly.

Murphy's doleful eyes looked from one detective to the other. "Doesn't it give me an alibi?"

"Miss Roach was murdered between seven and ten that evening, laddie," said King. "And you were probably only two hundred yards away well before ten."

"Were you?" asked Furnival.

Murphy hesitated. "Yes," he admitted finally. "I must have been back at the barn by half-past-nine."

"And you slept all night?"

"No, I didn't. I could tell something was wrong, that's why I bolted. I'd been lying in the straw for maybe an hour, but I couldn't get off to sleep so I thought I'd go outside and have a fag. I strolled up to a little hillock about fifty yards from the barn and I saw all these cars sweeping up the drive to the house. I couldn't think what was going on, it was too late for a party. After a bit I crept nearer, and I saw that three of the cars were police cars, and there was an ambulance, and searchlights set up in the garden, and policemen swarming all over the place. So I beat it back to my barn. I still wasn't really scared, but I thought I'd better not be discovered prowling around at midnight."

"You left the barn pretty early the next morning," said Furnival.

"Yes, I went before daylight. I thought it would be wiser. After all, the housekeeper had seen me watching the house."

"What did you do after you left?"

"I walked into Elmbridge and waited for the first bus to Meddenham. Then I hung around Meddenham all day waiting for the local paper to come out to see what had happened at the house. When I read about the old woman being killed, and how the police were looking for me, I was frightened out of my wits. I didn't know what to do—"

"You didn't think of coming in and making a statement?" Furnival asked.

"A bloke like me? Of no fixed abode!" Murphy laughed bitterly. "Ten years ago I might have done, but I've gone downhill a bit since those days. No, I went to the pictures—I felt safe in the dark. When I came out I bought some fish and chips. I went to the bus station to get a bus somewhere—a long distance bus—but I couldn't pluck up the nerve. I felt everybody was watching me. I started to walk out of town, but when I got into the suburbs I ran into a policeman. I was sure he was following me. Then I spotted that *House for Sale* board. It was dead easy to break in round the back. That's where I've been ever since. I was too frightened to come out, though all I had to eat was some chocolate from a machine. Honest to God, sir, I'm relieved you got me." Murphy slumped back in his chair as though he had got a weight off his mind.

"You didn't act relieved when Mrs. Booth found you," said King. "You were prepared to sell your life dearly."

"No! It wasn't like that! I just wanted to explain to her. I didn't want her to rush out screaming."

Furnival took Murphy's statement from King and read it through.

"Did you see anyone at any time hanging around Rowan Lodge?" he asked.

"I only saw the housekeeper and the lad who worked in the garden. But except for Sunday dinnertime and late Monday night I wasn't near the house."

"And you never went inside the house?"

"No!"

"You didn't help yourself to a porcelain figure?"

"A what?"

"A china figure of a man playing a violin?"

"Like a little statue," King added helpfully.

"What me? Are you kidding? I wouldn't have said no to a couple of quid, but what would I do with a china statue?"

"What, indeed?" sighed Furnival. "O.K., Murphy, that will do for now. Read it through, and if you agree it's what you said, sign it. If you think of anything else you want to say to me the gaoler will get hold of me."

He stood up. While King finished off the formalities of the statement and Murphy signed it, Furnival rang through to Peters and gave him the gist of what Murphy had said.

"What next?" Peters asked when Furnival had finished.

"Next we check it out," said Furnival.

"And it all checked out perfectly," Furnival said. "Every word the man uttered." He and Cantwell were sitting in

Cantwell's smart flat above the Elmbridge police station. Under his direction, more than twenty police officers, by telephone, by car, and on foot, had gone into every detail of Murphy's story. They had been to Blackett, to the farms where Murphy had failed to get work, to the *Black Cat* café, the *Foster Arms*, to lodging houses Murphy had used, and to a dozen other people and places. In addition Furnival had talked to Betty Booth to try and ascertain exactly what had happened in the empty house. Then he had driven out to Elmbridge, where, with Cantwell, he had gone through every statement looking for loose ends. Finally they had retired upstairs where young Mrs. Cantwell brewed them coffee.

"What sort of a chap is he?" Cantwell asked.

"Seen better days," said Furnival. "Haven't they always? He's a widower, no kids. He seems to have worked fairly steadily until his wife died seven years ago, he went to the dogs a bit after that. Everyone speaks quite well of him, he's a drifter and doesn't stay long in a job, but he doesn't give any trouble. Same story in the lodging houses, he's quiet, keeps himself to himself, never makes trouble."

"He attacked that girl," said Cantwell.

"He didn't attack her. All she has is a couple of bruises on her arms. A man that size could have killed her with ease if he'd wanted to."

"Why would she lie?"

"She wasn't lying. She told it as it seemed to her. I've just come from her home, they've got a couple of rooms in her parents' house. I should imagine that Betty Booth had a sheltered upbringing with gentle parents. Now she has a nice husband to spoil her. I don't suppose she's seen a fist, or heard a voice, raised in anger in her life. How do you think she would react to this big scruffy man rushing at her?"

"Ooh, I should have been petrified!" Iris Cantwell shuddered delicately. She passed Furnival his coffee in a fine china cup with a linen napkin. Furnival guessed that whatever the hour one would never get slapdash housekeeping in her house. He hadn't much taken to young Mrs. Cantwell, who struck him as smug, prim and far too unadaptable to make a good policeman's wife. He glanced at Cantwell's flaming hair and reckless eyes and thought there could be trouble there.

"Sleeping rough like that!" she was going on. "Ugh, you ought to lock up people like that."

Cantwell looked slightly embarrassed. "You're holding him I suppose?" he said to Furnival.

"Oh, Lord, yes. We've booked him for breaking and entering, and there's assault if Mrs. Booth wants to press charges. We can hang on to him for a bit, but, as I say, everything he told us has been verified. Even the unobservant Len Carver remembers him travelling on the first bus into Meddenham on Tuesday morning."

"He doesn't need to lie about all that," said Cantwell. "It isn't relevant. Nobody can alibi him between nine and ten on Monday night. He could have done everything he said and still have murdered Miss Roach between those times."

"But *why*?" demanded Furnival. "What possible motive did he have?"

"That china figure is missing—"

"If you ask me, that Meissen theft stinks to high heaven. By a vagrant? A vagrant named *Murphy*? He certainly had nothing on him, and there was nothing hidden in the barn. Anyway, don't forget that Miss Roach let her murderer into the house herself."

"Unless he concealed himself in the house earlier," said Cantwell.

"Then it wasn't Murphy. We have him alibied until nine o'clock."

There was a silence while the tired men racked their brains.

"Perhaps he told some really plausible story at the door and Miss Roach let him in," suggested Cantwell. "We know she wasn't nervous."

"She wasn't crazy either. This wasn't a shop where anyone can walk in. Why should she let him in? And then resume her seat? It doesn't make sense. In any case, the method is wrong. An intruder would have bashed her, or even throttled her, he wouldn't have smothered her."

There was another pause. Iris Cantwell pressed more coffee on them brightly. Furnival felt himself getting sleepy. He humped himself upright on the deep sofa.

"We mustn't forget both George Shannon and Miss Bennett lied about their movements, and they both stand to inherit. We have to find out whether their lies are important, and I think while we do it we'll let them think we're quite happy with Murphy."

"But you're not really satisfied he did it, are you?" pressed Cantwell. "You think he's innocent."

"I think it's a pity he didn't stay in that pub till closing time," said Furnival.

CHAPTER TEN

MATTHEW FURNIVAL slept until eight the following morning, then yelled at his wife Joanna for letting him do so.

"Nonsense," said Joanna, uncontrite. She pushed him back against the pillows, and thrust a cup of tea in his hand. "You have to get some rest, you only had two hours sleep on Monday night, and you were up before six yesterday. Surely it can wait for a few minutes now. After all, you've got your man."

Furnival took a couple of gulps of the scalding tea, got out of bed and started groping around for his slippers. "It's not all cut and dried," he said testily. "There isn't a shred of evidence against the man."

"Oh, you always have to have it difficult," said Joanna. She slipped out of her housecoat and started to dress rapidly.

"Good God, what am I supposed to do? Grab any poor bastard who happened to be in the neighbourhood? Do you realise there could have been a dozen transient farm workers sleeping out near Rowan Lodge that night? It was merely that Miss Bennett happened to spot Murphy. Where the hell are my slippers?"

Joanna extricated them from beneath the wardrobe. "Some detective!" she said sweetly.

They ate a hasty breakfast at the counter Furnival had built in the kitchen. Joanna was on her morning duty at a charity shop in the centre of Meddenham and was also in a hurry to be off.

"What are you going to be doing today?" she asked her husband.

"I'm going out to look for Sid Robbins. I know it's stupid—I don't know the country, and there are a hundred things I'd be better employed doing—but I feel that I must. It's as though he had disappeared off the face of the earth."

Furnival got his things together, while Joanna put on her suede jacket and adjusted a little tweed hat over her black curls. He gave her a lift to her shop, and as she got out noticed a line of ladies waiting inside for her arrival.

"Don't talk about the case, darling," he said.

Joanna leant in and kissed him. "You don't have to caution me."

Furnival picked up King at his home and together they drove to Elmbridge. He dropped King at the station then went on alone to Sid Robbins' home.

He was shocked by Mrs. Robbins' appearance. Her skin was a greyish-white, and there were deep bruised circles beneath her dull eyes. She sat in the little front room staring through the grimy lace curtains, her fingers incessantly twisting at her apron. Three or four dirty small children were yelling and squabbling around her feet.

"Sid hasn't been home to see you?" Furnival asked her. He had thought that the lad might have managed to visit his home after dark, but one look at Mrs. Robbins told him that he was wrong.

She shook her head hopelessly. "I don't think I'll ever see him again," she said.

"What do you think has happened to him?"

"I think he's drowned. He always liked to hang around the river and it's running so fast now."

"Could he support himself for nearly three days if he was hiding out in the country?"

"I dunno. I suppose he might, he's quite handy. He could get eggs and fish and make a fire. The only thing is, he don't like to pinch things like a normal boy. But, if he's alive, why haven't you found him, Mr. Furnival? There's so many policemen looking—"

"I don't know, Mrs. Robbins. I wish I did."

"Are you going to hang our Sid when you catch him?" enquired a small girl who Furnival dimly recognised as Angela.

"No, no," he protested. "We just want to look after him, and see that he's warm and dry and has something to eat."

He sorted out the biggest lad from the crowd of children.

"What's your name, son?"

"Gerald, sir."

"Well, Gerald, did you ever go anywhere with Sid? Did he have any special places he liked to go?"

"I never went out with him." The boy ran his hand through his matted carroty hair. "My pals said he was daft."

Tears welled up in Mrs. Robbins' big dark eyes and slowly crept down her cheeks.

"I loved him, sir," she whispered. "I loved him best of all."

" I know, we heard he was a sweet-natured lad," said Furnival. " Give me his doctor's address, I'll go and have a word with him. Shouldn't this lot be at school," he added as the uproar in the room grew deafening.

" It's their half-term, sir."

" Well, couldn't they play outside? It's a lovely morning and they look as though they could do with some fresh air."

The boy shuffled his feet. " People shout after us," he muttered. " They say our Sid's a murderer. They throw stones."

Oh God, it's started, thought Furnival. " Have you had your breakfast?" he asked. The children shook their heads dumbly. " If you're so smart, get them something to eat," he said to Gerald. " You can get some cornflakes, or something, can't you? And after that go out and get some chocolate." He gave the boy half-a-crown.

" You may find things get a bit better," he said to Mrs. Robbins. " We've got a man in custody—"

" Is he the murderer?"

" I can't tell you anything more. But it may take the pressure off you a bit. I'm going out now to look for Sid. I'll come in to see you again." He closed the door on the racket of Gerald supervising in the kitchen, and walked back up the High Street to the address of Sid's doctor.

It proved to be a pleasant, rather shabby, Victorian house. Dr. Swinney, who was taking surgery, agreed to see him straight away. The doctor, like his house, was pleasant and somewhat shabby, with flowing white hair, keen blue eyes, and a full-blown rose in the buttonhole of his ancient tweed suit.

" Sid Robbins?" he said when Furnival had stated his

business. "I can't say I've had a lot to do with him personally—he has excellent physical health—but I know the family well. The younger ones always have something or other, and the mother is somewhat inadequate. I looked in to see her yesterday and left her something to help her sleep, but I don't suppose she'll take it until Sid is found. She's going through a bad time."

"It could get worse when Sid is found."

"You mean if he's guilty?"

"I was going to ask your opinion. Could he be guilty of murder?"

Dr. Swinney took off his spectacles and shone them on a pocket handkerchief.

"I don't know," he said after a minute. "I simply don't know. It certainly never occurred to me that he would hurt anybody. I always thought of him as just an ordinary kid, like her others. But Sid is twenty, you see, and they are under twelve."

"I believe he's been known to lose his temper with people who upset him."

"Don't we all? I can't say I ever heard of much trouble with him. He's childish, of course, and moody, but he isn't vicious. He boarded at a special school until he was fifteen, he was very happy there, and he liked working for Miss Roach. Discipline suits him, and he had a friend and ally in Miss Bennett."

"There was some bother on Monday and Miss Roach was sharp with him. Might he have killed her if she was scolding him again at night? Smothered her perhaps to stop the harsh words."

The doctor looked suddenly older. "It's glib," he said. "My profession distrusts glibness, but it's possible. I'm not a specialist, I don't know the way his mind might work, but I would say it was out of character."

Furnival thanked him and left the surgery. He walked back to the police station where Cantwell was organising a hunt for Sid a few miles up river where the country merged into moorland. Furnival checked with Meddenham that there were no urgent calls for him, then with King he followed the car with the three local men out of town. As they passed the turn for Rowan Lodge he told King about his depressing morning.

"Mrs. Robbins is near the end of her tether. She's had such a rotten deal, her husband disabled for years, then dying and leaving her with all those kids—the oldest a near idiot—and now this! And if that wasn't enough, it looks as though the neighbours are turning nasty."

King looked at him. "And you want Sid to turn up, safe and well and innocent, claim his two hundred quid inheritance, blow them all to new clothes and toys, and live happily ever after?"

"And you don't, I suppose?"

"It's no good getting too involved—Whoa up! They're turning off."

Just ahead of them the police car had turned down a minor road on the left. They followed it for about a mile before it stopped in a small hamlet, a mere dozen poor cottages and a derelict chapel. Furnival and King got out and joined the uniformed policemen, two of them young and one middle-aged. A group of children at once materialised and stood gaping at them.

"This is Shalebeach, sir," said the older man. "We'll have to leave the cars here."

"Is there anything special about this place?" Furnival

asked. " I mean, is it a likely place for Robbins to come?"

" Lads have always come here. The river is pretty and there are plenty of fish, and lots of caves and hidey holes. I came here often when I was a kid." The middle-aged policeman got the walkie-talkie sets and binoculars from the car and handed them round.

" Have you been out looking for Robbins every day?" asked Furnival.

" Yes, since early Tuesday morning. We were looking for the other man as well at first, the one you caught yesterday. Now it's only Robbins."

" Have you used dogs?"

" Yes. They've got the dogs over at Woberton today. I don't see how he's eluded us out here in the open, and his mother doesn't seem to think he'd go near a town. Sergeant Cantwell says the Chief Constable was talking of dragging the river."

The five men walked up the macadam lane to where it petered out about half a mile from the village. In front of them the moor spread out as far as eye could see and through the middle of it the river wound its way. On the skyline was a ridge of young forest, a dozen shades of green and gold and brown blending together like tweed. At first glance the flattish moorland offered little concealment, but after studying it for a few minutes Furnival realised there were many places—wooded hollows, dense crops of bracken, ruined stone feedstores—where a man could hide.

The five policemen separated and each started to work a portion down to the river. Much of it could be cleared at a glance, the grass was cropped low by the sheep and there were no impediments except small boulders; but the tall clumps of gorse had to be pushed aside, step by step, tearing at their hands and ankles, and there were several lengthy detours to possible hiding places.

By two o'clock Furnival was hot and weary and footsore from scrambling over the stony outcrops. To add to his discomfort his feet were soaking from misjudged footholds on the river-bank. He had disturbed nothing except a score of birds and rabbits. He gave a signal to the others and they came together beside the river. Furnival threw his coat, which he had been carrying, on the ground and sat on it.

"Got to have a breather," he explained. "Has anybody spotted anything?"

"Not a thing," said the older policeman whose name was Sperry, "Not even a print. Apart from last Monday it's been dry for weeks. Might as well have our sandwiches now, we'll get over the river and do that side after we've eaten. You can ford across down there."

The men ate in silence, then lit up cigarettes to discourage the clouds of flies that rose up out of the bracken. The day had begun with bright October sunshine, but it had clouded over now and a chill raw mist had drifted down. Over the whole moor there was no sound except for the bleating of sheep, and the desolate call of a curlew. Furnival shivered.

The afternoon was much the same as the morning, except that the other side of the river was steeper and rougher. Furnival scrambled and sweated, slithered and cursed, his way along his portion of the river bank and across the open country to the edge of the wood which was to serve as the boundary to that day's search. After a further two hours he decided he had had enough and hailing the men he told them he was going back to Meddenham. King decided to stay with the hunt a bit longer and return with the other men. Furnival was a considerable distance from the cars, and even jog-trotting the whole way it took him almost half an hour to reach Shalebeach where he was heartily glad to sink into the leathery warmth of the car.

CHAPTER ELEVEN

FURNIVAL DROVE through Elmbridge without stopping, but, on impulse, turned into the forecourt of the Country Club.

It was five-thirty, the dead hour at the club. In the lounge two gentlemen with heads back and mouth gaping were sleeping off the effects of unwise luncheons. From the almost deserted billiard room came the thin click of balls. Furnival looked around and spotted the barman he had spoken to previously, polishing glasses behind the bar. He squelched his way across to him, conscious of his sodden shoes on the expensive carpet.

The barman greeted him warily. "I'm sorry to bother you again," Furnival said. "But I have an hour's discrepancy between the time Mrs. Shannon says her husband left home on Monday night and the time you say he arrived here. I don't suppose for a moment it has anything to do with my business but I have to check it out." He attempted a man-of-the-world leer. "I wondered—perhaps—a girl-friend?"

The barman satisfied himself with the shine on the glass he was holding and lined it up with its fellows. "The gentlemen here rely on my discretion," he said carefully.

"I realise that. But it was awkward for Mr. Shannon, his wife was present while I was questioning him, you know how it is? Now I don't want to start a full scale investigation over a little point that could be cleared up in a few minutes."

"Well, it's true Mr. Shannon has got a lady friend," said the man. "He's brought her in here once or twice."

"Sure it wasn't his wife?"

"No, I've seen his wife. This was a younger lady, with dark hair. He called her Gwen."

"Was she with him on Monday?"

"No, sir. Like I said, he came in at nine o'clock and he was alone."

"Thank you." Furnival turned to go. "By the way, who put Shannon up for membership. Do members have to be sponsored?"

"Oh, certainly, sir. As I recall it Mr. Baer sponsored Mr. Shannon. That's the gentleman who has the antique shop in Elmbridge. He's a foreign gentleman, but very pleasant."

"Yes, I've met him. Were he and Shannon friendly?"

"Not that you'd notice. Of course, Mr. Baer was one of our earliest members, he joined soon after we opened ten years ago. Mr. Shannon has only been a member for four or five months. But it's funny, now you come to mention it, I only ever saw them together once and they didn't look very friendly then."

"Were they quarrelling?"

"No. Mr. Shannon was doing nearly all the talking. He talked for—oh—half an hour, and Mr. Baer looked sicker and sicker. He just put in a few words now and again as though he was protesting. When he got up and left I said to Charlie who was on with me—' Mr. Baer looks as if he'd been put through a wringer'."

"Can you remember when this took place?"

"It would be, let me see—Charlie and me on, Rosa off—" The barman made a few muttered calculations involving the staff rota. "It would be a week ago last Monday."

Exactly one week before the murder. It had probably no relevance whatever, but Furnival was always intrigued when people acted out of character. Shannon and Baer had appeared to have little contact, then, just a week before the murder, there had been this lengthy conversation that seemed to upset Baer. It had better not be ignored. Furnival thought longingly of a hot meal and dry socks. He looked in the mirror behind the barman's head. Even its calculatedly kindly rosy tint could not disguise his dishevelled appearance. "Can I use the men's room?" he said.

Furnival washed his face and hands in the club's superbly appointed washroom and dragged a comb through his matted hair. Then having brushed a few heather fronds from his clothes and adjusted his tie he turned back to Elmbridge once more.

It was just after six o'clock on the market hall clock as he drove down the High Street and all the shops were either closed or closing. He parked the car and walked into St. Stephen's Row to find that all three shops there were closed. He knocked at Baer's door and waited, then knocked again more loudly. There was no answer. He decided to ask the helpful Miss Wittering if she knew Baer's whereabouts when the door of the café opened and Baer himself came out, a cake box under his arm. He started slightly when he saw Furnival, but immediately recovered himself.

"I have been treating myself," he indicated the box. "Coffee cake for tea. Miss Wittering makes coffee cake like a Viennese. Were you waiting for me?"

"Yes. Could we go inside?"

Baer unlocked his door and the two men went through the shop to the office. Baer put his cake down on the filing cabinet and waved Furnival to a chair. "What can I do for you?"

"How well do you know George Shannon?" Furnival began abruptly.

Baer looked surprised. "Scarcely at all."

"You sponsored him for membership of the Elmbridge Country Club."

"Oh, that, yes. He asked me if I would put him forward, and I knew his aunt slightly— It's just a formality. All the Elmbridge really wants to know is whether one can pay their subs."

"Apart from that, you didn't have much to do with him?"

"No, he struck me as a rather shallow young man. I thought he could become a bore."

Furnival glanced at Baer's face. As far as he could tell the man was mildly intrigued by his questions, nothing more. He took his notebook from his pocket. "We have a record of a conversation you had with Mr. Shannon at the Country Club on the evening of the Monday before last. A conversation that lasted about half an hour."

It brought all the reaction Furnival could have wished. Baer's tanned skin turned greyish colour and he looked ten years older in an instant.

"What do you mean?" he whispered. "You have a record?"

"I mean you were overheard."

"If we were overheard you will know I refused to have anything to do with his proposition."

"What was his proposition?"

Baer hesitated. "Come along," Furnival said. "This is a murder investigation and Shannon is a possible suspect. If you had prior knowledge—"

"Not of murder!" Baer's voice shook. "It was nothing to do with murder."

"Then what? Was Shannon asking you to do something? I really think you'd better tell me."

There was another pause, then Baer said, "He wanted me to dispose of his aunt's Meissen figures."

Furnival was surprised. "You mean the singer and the violinist? But they aren't worth very much."

"Shannon thought they were, and I had never seen them."

"What did he intend to do? Steal them?"

"Yes. And I was in effect to act as a 'fence'."

"Why on earth did he involve a second person? Particularly if you were no more than acquaintances."

"I suppose he thought I had the professional outlets."

"What I really meant was why should he imagine that you, a reputable businessman, would go along with such a scheme?"

Again Baer was silent. Furnival watched his face, shadowy and distorted, in the old convex mirror on the wall. "Did he have some sort of hold over you?" he asked softly.

Baer wrung his hands in an unEnglish gesture of despair. "It was ten years ago," he said. "I thought it was all forgotten. And I was innocent, no case was ever brought against me." He stopped at Furnival's mystified face.

"You remember the Coverdale Hall robbery?" he said.

Furnival did not *remember* it. He had not been on the Meddenham force for very long, and as Baer had said, it had occurred ten years earlier. But it was impossible to be connected with the Meddenham police without constant reminders of the Coverdale job, the biggest haul ever made in that part of the country. It had been mostly silver, a large part of it still unrecovered, and when any items turned up from rather suspect sources they still had to be checked against the lists of the missing Coverdale Hall stuff.

"I know about it," Furnival said. "How were you involved?"

"I bought some of the stuff. Some candlesticks, a salver, and a coffee service. I had no idea it was stolen, but I'll admit I didn't enquire into proof of ownership as thoroughly as I should have done; and the men accepted such a low figure that I should have suspected their *bona fides*. But I wasn't so experienced then. and I needed a quick profit so badly; I was just getting my business on its feet." The face in the mirror seemed to dissolve in old shadows. "The next day the news story broke in the papers." Baer went on. "I realised immediately that I was involved, but I did not dare to go to the police. Three days later they came to me. They searched my place and found the stuff."

"What happened?" asked Furnival.

"I helped them all I could. I gave them descriptions of the men involved—"

"A bit belated."

"I realised that. The men were never caught. The police came within a hair's breadth of charging me with receiving, but finally I was able to convince them that I had acted in innocence."

"I think you were very lucky," said Furnival when Baer had finished his story.

"I was innocent, but—yes, I was lucky, too. If it had come out I would have been finished in this community, and in the trade. This is a precarious business at any time, and I was more vulnerable than most. I was a German, not even a refugee. I had fought against this country."

"And Shannon had somehow dug all this up? I wonder how? He wasn't even in Elmbridge ten years ago; it was about that time that his aunt was attacked and I remember him telling me that he was living in London. And why has he waited till now to make use of it?"

"I know how Shannon knew about it, Inspector. He had the forms that I made my statement on."

"*What?*"

"The old police records of my statements. I made several—they must have run to thousands of words. He showed them to me."

"But—how did he come to have them?"

"He found them somewhere in his house when he was converting it. It used to be the police station."

Furnival was horrified. "But that's appalling. They should never have been left lying around for the public to find. Who took your statements at the time? Can you remember?"

"Could I ever forget it? It was Sergeant Wainwright."

"I had heard that his reports were in a mess, but not that he was so disgracefully careless. I'm very sorry that this happened. However, let's come up to date now to the Monday of last week. What exactly happened? Did Shannon accost you in the Country Club waving your statements?"

"Not quite," Baer smiled weakly. "He thought he was being rather suave. He began by complimenting me on the prosperous business I had built up. Then he said that he might be able to put some business my way. He wanted a really good offer for his aunt's pair of Meissen figures. Naturally I was interested. Miss Roach's Meissen figures had acquired a local reputation despite the fact that no one outside her family had ever seen them. I told him that I was surprised she wanted to sell, and then he came out into the open and said that she was to know nothing about it. He intended to help himself to the figures. They would be coming to him eventually, he said, and he needed the money now."

"I simply couldn't believe my ears," Baer went on. "I thought he was joking. I thought he was drunk! To be speaking coolly of this to a mere acquaintance! For a few minutes I kidded along with him, then I realised he was in earnest and I stood up to go. He pulled me down again by my sleeve, and showed me the statements in his pockets."

"I take it violence was not mentioned?" Furnival said.

"No. He was just going to filch the figures."

"And you refused to collaborate?"

"Absolutely."

"But only one figure has gone. He spoke of two?"

"I'm sure he meant both of them. But he may have planned to take one at a time, hoping they would not be missed. Or he may have had the fiddler valued elsewhere and found out that it was worth very little."

"Yes, that's possible. Although to hope that Miss Roach wouldn't notice its disappearance seems a bit naïve. He never spoke of this again to you, either before or after his aunt's death?"

"Not a word. When he saw that I would have nothing to do with it he tried to make a joke of it. He said my murky past would be safe with him."

Furnival got up. "Thanks, Mr. Baer. I'll see that your statements are retrieved and destroyed—as they should have been years ago. In this country men don't have to live with ancient indiscretions all their lives."

He made his way through the shop and let himself out. From the street he looked back at Baer still standing in his office doorway. He did not look as if he would enjoy his coffee cake.

Furnival walked slowly back to the police station. He would have liked a little time on his own to puzzle over this new development. Cantwell was undoubtedly keen and intelligent, and for a young and inexperienced officer he had organised the Elmbridge end of the inquiry most efficiently. But he did show a tendency to jump to conclusions, and Furnival, as Joanna had remarked, liked things the hard way.

He found Cantwell in his front office with the desk officer and a cadet. The sergeant was wearing a raincoat and muddy gumboots and he looked tired.

"Any luck?" Furnival asked.

Cantwell shook his head wearily. "Not a trace. We've been around Woberton and Ashton all day. I've just sent the dogs back and dispersed the men. The light was going."

"What about King and the others at Shalebeach?"

"Fraser says they checked in just before us. They've gone off now for a meal and some rest. They didn't find anything. I don't know how the lad is surviving, the nights are very cold." Cantwell dragged off his boots and padded into his own office. "By the way, there was a message for you five minutes ago. The forensic lab have finished tests on Murphy's clothes. They found nothing on them."

"I suppose there need not be, there was no actual physical contact during the killing. Something rather odd has come up here, though. It could be important. I haven't thought it out." Furnival closed the door to the office and recounted Baer's story.

Cantwell was almost comically horrified. "That stupid bastard Wainwright, he should be charged!"

"It was appallingly careless."

"And what a swine Shannon must be, to drag up a man's past when he's trying to make something of himself."

"It's as nasty a method of blackmail as I've ever come across, and there must be quite a few charges we could get him on. But the important thing at the moment is how it affects our case."

Cantwell simmered down. "It brings the china figure in again," he said. "And I didn't believe it had any connection with the murder."

"Neither did I. I thought it had simply been broken. But if ten days ago Shannon was planning to steal it, and four days ago it was gone, there's a strong chance he had it. So assuming the theft, why the murder? He had got away with the first figure, he didn't have to kill to get that. Was he after the second?"

"He knew Miss Bennett was out on Monday nights," put in Cantwell.

"But his aunt would be there, he couldn't hope to walk in and help himself. Perhaps Miss Roach telephoned him and asked him to call on her on Monday night, and during the visit she told him she suspected him of stealing the fiddler. She had told Miss Bennett she suspected the Shannons. Perhaps she took a tough line with him—threatened to call the police. Anyway, let's pay him a call. There are all sorts of possibilities to put the fear of God into him!"

Cantwell laced on his shoes and fetched an empty box-file from the cupboard. "While we're there I'll collect all those old police records he hoped to make a living from." He smiled grimly. "Shannon—yes I like that very much!"

Furnival grinned. "Well, don't go off half-cocked! I also discovered he has a girl-friend, he may simply have been with her. You liked Murphy, remember!"

"Shannon is better. I forget what proportion of murders are committed by the victim's own family, but I know it beats vagrants any day!"

CHAPTER TWELVE

FURNIVAL AND Cantwell walked together to the old station house. It was eight o'clock and almost completely dark. In the second before Furnival banged the knocker they heard the voices of the two Shannons raised in argument inside. The door was opened by George Shannon looking flushed and sulky.

"Oh, it's you again," he said grudgingly. "I can't spare long. It's my aunt's funeral on Saturday and there are still arrangements to be made." He stood aside. "Well, come in, come in!"

They all crowded into the small lounge. "You'll know Sergeant Cantwell," Furnival said. "He's your local man."

"Not professionally!" Shannon laughed loudly and extended a hand to Cantwell who managed to ignore it without offence. "Well, let's get down to business. Is it about that silly slip my wife made over the time I went out on Monday?"

"No, my visit isn't connected with your aunt's death, Mr. Shannon," said Furnival. "It's about some old police records that may have been left behind here when the station was moved."

Laura Shannon gave a nervous giggle of relief. "Oh, is *that* all! I thought—" She hurried on, "There was *loads* of stuff here when we moved in. Was it important? I'm afraid the children have crayoned over some of it." While Laura prattled on, Furnival looked at George Shannon. Unlike his wife he did not seem relieved at Furnival's mission, but was regarding the policeman apprehensively.

"Mrs. Shannon, would you round up everything you can find and give it to Sergeant Cantwell?" said Furnival. "I'm sorry to put you to so much trouble, but we don't want the stuff falling into the wrong hands."

Laura went out of the room followed by Cantwell. Furnival allowed the silence to lengthen until Shannon said, clearing his throat, "Why is a C.I.D. inspector taking time off from a murder case to chase up a lot of old forms?"

"I think you know the answer to that, Mr. Shannon," said Furnival. "I think those forms fell into very wrong hands and you used them to try to coerce a man into committing a felony."

"It was only a joke," said Shannon sullenly. "Just a joke to take the wind out of Mr. bloody Baer's sails. You get so sick of these foreigners coming over here and making fortunes out of us. You should have seen the place he had fifteen years ago when I was a kid. A poky little junk shop near my aunt's shop. And now he's in the middle of the High Street and lording it around the Country Club."

"So you thought you would involve him in a crime?"

"He was involved in a crime. I read all that stuff about the Coverdale Hall robbery. And he got away with it! I reckon he had pull with you lot!"

Furnival regarded Shannon with distaste. "We'll leave aside for a moment the charges that can be brought against you over this business. How did you dispose of Miss Roach's Dresden figure after Baer had refused to collaborate?"

"I didn't dispose of it. I never had it. I dropped the whole idea when Baer wouldn't play along. It was partly a lark anyway, I was a bit tight at the time. I was fed up. Aunt Grace had been such a mean old bitch to me all her life. She would never buy me a car, she wouldn't help us with the house, and there were her precious Meissen figures so easily portable." Shannon mopped at his brow. "I thought Baer did that sort of thing all the time. If you'd read that evidence you would have thought he was an experienced fence! But when he wouldn't have anything to do with it I just forgot the whole thing. I couldn't have found a customer on my own."

"You could have found a more pliant dealer."

"I hadn't got anything on any other dealers."

"You could have offered them a percentage."

"Well, I didn't. I never touched the thing, thank God. I hear it's nearly valueless. I would have looked a mug!"

Furnival leant back in his chair and regarded Shannon blandly. "Hard to believe, Shannon, the figure mysteriously disappearing the day your aunt was murdered. I don't like coincidences."

"What about the man you arrested?"

"Murphy? I don't think we're going to be able to pin it on him."

"Well, it was nothing to do with me," Shannon said sulkily. "I wouldn't have dared to pinch the figure. My aunt would have suspected me, anyway."

"I think she did suspect you. I think she sent for you and threatened to expose you."

"No! No! I thought you'd got Murphy."

"I told you, I don't think we can pin it on him, or on poor old Sid. They had no motive, you see. We like a motive."

There was a silence. Shannon sunk his head on his hands. After a minute he raised it and looked at Furnival wretchedly. "What did you say about charges? I'm sure if I talked to Bill Baer he wouldn't want to press charges. After all—a fellow club member."

"I can't answer for Mr. Baer," Furnival said shortly. "Did you get any other bright ideas from your reading of those official forms?"

"No, the rest was very dull stuff. Mostly traffic offences. It was just that my little girl showed me a drawing she had done on a form, and Baer's name caught my eye. I got interested and gathered up all the rest of the evidence I could find. I couldn't find it all, but I found enough."

"Hand it over," Furnival said.

Shannon extracted an envelope from his breast pocket and handed it to Furnival.

"Is this the lot?"

"It's all I found."

From outside the door they heard Cantwell and Laura's voices.

"I'll just have Gwen's address, then," said Furnival suddenly.

Shannon's mouth dropped open, "What?"

"Gwen. Your girl-friend. Or perhaps Mrs. Shannon would know?"

Shannon glared at him. "20, Brunswick Terrace, Meddenham," he gabbled.

"Name?"

"Lomax."

Cantwell and Laura came into the room. Furnival was amused to notice Cantwell's air of flirtatious gallantry to which Laura Shannon was responding with flattered giggles.

Shannon scowled at his wife. " What's the matter with you? What is there to be giggling like a schoolgirl about?"

Laura sobered. " I'm sorry, George. Mr. Cantwell was showing me how the handcuffs worked, and then he pretended he didn't have the key!" She turned to Furnival. " We found all this stuff, Mr. Furnival. There may be more in the children's rooms, I'll have a look tomorrow." She emptied the contents of her arms on to the table and Cantwell did the same. In addition to a large quantity of papers, most of them yellowed with age, there were rubber stamps, badges, a pair of handcuffs, and a helmet. " They're going to miss the helmet," she smiled.

Furnival pushed it to one side. " Have it on me," he said.

Cantwell stuffed all the papers into the file he had brought with him. " I'll take these back to the station and go through them," he said. " Maybe Sergeant Wainwright will have a look at them with me. I expect most of them can be destroyed." He bundled the other items into his pockets and smiled at Laura. " I'll call in tomorrow if I may, to see if you've found anything else."

Furnival accompanied Cantwell to the door. "And I'll let you know what action we'll be taking in the matter," he said to Shannon.

George Shannon closed the door on them and turned on his wife. " You were making a bit of a fool of yourself with Cantwell, weren't you? Proper cheap you looked, tittering up at him. He may have married old Barnaby's daughter, but he's only a bloody copper you know!"

" I'm sorry, George. I suppose I was nervous, and he was so nice to me. I thought if we were friendly with him—"

" You needn't think flirting with him is going to get us preferential treatment. In any case he isn't going to look at you. His own wife is a sight smarter *and* she's got money!"

Laura turned away so that George should not see how much he had hurt her. " But why should we need preferential treatment? We haven't done anything." She looked back at her husband's face. " George, what did the inspector mean when he said he'd let you know what action he'd be taking in the matter? What matter?"

" It was nothing important. It was about—clearing up Aunt Grace's stuff."

" But why would the police take action about that?" Two lines etched themselves in Laura's smooth brow. " George, you're lying to me, like you lied about not leaving home till eight-thirty on Monday. You *know* you left at half-past-seven."

" Shut up! Do you want them to arrest me? Christ, what a wife! If a wife can't believe in her husband—"

Laura crossed the room and attempted to put her arms around her husband who pettishly turned away. " George, you know I'd stand by you in anything. I'd lie for you. But you can't ask me to believe what didn't happen." Laura hesitated, " Were you with a girl?"

George Shannon flung away. " Oh, don't start that again! You've got other women on the brain. Not that I wouldn't have every excuse. You whine and nag from morning till night, you let yourself go—"

Laura closed her eyes tightly. " I wish it was a girl. Anything would be better than this uncertainty."

Shannon looked at his wife in amazement. " Good God, Laura, you think I killed the old girl!"

Laura opened her eyes and two tears trickled down her cheeks. " You said there would be a bit of money soon," she whispered. " Don't you remember? We were coming home from Aunt Grace's two Sundays ago, and I said I was tired of going in the same old coat every week, and you said there'd be a bit of money soon."

" No, I don't remember. I expect I said it to shut you up. You don't think I killed her for ten quid for a new coat?"

" It was the way you said it," Laura persisted. " As though an idea had just struck you." Two more tears launched themselves. " I haven't been able to get it out of my mind."

" You poor little darling!" George gathered Laura in his arms just like they did it on the telly. " You've had a rotten time. Look, have a day out in Meddenham tomorrow, it will be a change for you." He extracted a pound note from his wallet with a flourish. " Get yourself some lunch with this."

" Oh, George!" Laura looked up bright-eyed. " How sweet of you." She stopped. " But I forgot, Mr. Cantwell is coming back tomorrow. I'd better wait until Monday."

" Damn Cantwell. He can call any time, it's only a few yards. Aren't the schools on holiday this week? Why not get one of those highschool girls to have the kids for the day?"

Laura wavered. " That would be marvellous. Do you think it would be all right?"

" Of course. In fact I insist," said George masterfully. He huddled over his wallet again. " Here. Here's ten quid. Get yourself a coat for the funeral."

"Oh, George!" said Laura. She snuggled into her husband's ample shoulder. "You are good to me. I'm sorry I said what I did about another woman."

George kissed Laura's tousled blonde head. "Silly girl," he said, "as if I would!"

"Miss Gwen Lomax?" enquired Furnival.

The girl in the doorway of 20, Brunswick Terrace nodded dumbly. She was small and dark and looked about eighteen.

"I'm from the police. Can I have a word with you?"

The girl glanced nervously over her shoulder.

"Gwen! Gwen! Who is it?" a man's harsh voice demanded from the back of the house.

Miss Lomax rolled her eyes at Furnival imploringly. "It's just someone from business, Dad," she called.

"Well, ask him in, can't you?"

With another pleading glance at Furnival the girl led the way down the narrow passage to a brightly lit kitchen. In the better light Furnival saw that Gwen Lomax was exceedingly pretty and her brief wool dress revealed excellent legs and figure. He turned his gaze reluctantly on Mr. Lomax, who sat at the table the epitome of the English proletarian father, collarless shirt open at the neck, a knife and fork in his huge fists, a glass of beer and a varied array of sauce bottles at his elbow.

He ducked his head civilly at Furnival. "Good evening, sir. I hope my little girl hasn't been misbehaving herself?"

"Oh—no, Mr. Lomax. Certainly not," said Furnival weakly.

"I'm glad to hear it. Her mam and I were that pleased when she got herself a job with the insurance. But then, she always was a bright girl."

"Dad, it's business," Gwen Lomax broke in. "Can we use the front room?"

"You may," said her father. "Don't forget to turn the light out when you've done." He nodded again at Furnival, and conveyed a large portion of chop to his mouth.

Gwen led Furnival down the passage to a cold and comfortless front room and switched on one bar of the small electric fire.

"Thank you for not letting on you were the police," she whispered.

"Your father doesn't know of your relationship with George Shannon?"

"Oh, no, he'd kill me! You won't have to tell him, will you?"

"Miss Lomax, I only want to talk to *you*. Of course, it may have to come out later."

Gwen huddled in a chair near the fire. "I suppose his wife put you on to us? Well, she can't get a divorce through me. George and I didn't—you know—do anything."

Furnival stared at her. "Why do you imagine I am here?"

"Isn't it because George and I were going together?"

"I think you're confusing me with a private enquiry agent. That sort of thing is not the business of the police. I'm enquiring into the death of Mr. Shannon's aunt, Miss Roach."

"Oh, *that*!" Miss Lomax's relief was plain. "I read all about it in the paper. Wasn't it *dreadful*? And then to go and attack that poor girl in the empty house!"

"Have you seen Mr. Shannon since it happened?"

" No. I rang him up at his office yesterday morning, but he was at the inquest."

" When did you last see him?"

" On Monday evening."

In his mind's eye Furnival reluctantly struck George Shannon's name from his list, seeing the figure of Sid Robbins getting lonelier and lonelier in the centre of the arena.

" What time was this?"

" It was at ten to eight."

" You're sure?"

" Yes, I was waiting for him. I was looking at my watch."

" Where was this?"

" In Meddenham. The *Silver Grill* café. It's near the library."

" Yes, I know it." The café was on the Elmbridge side of Meddenham, and twenty minutes for the drive from Shannon's house was just about right. " What time did Mr. Shannon leave?"

" At ten past eight. We just had a cup of coffee."

" That's a long drive for a cup of coffee and twenty minutes chat." Furnival smiled at the girl. " He must be very fond of you."

" I didn't expect him to leave so early," the girl said. " I thought we were going to spend the evening together. But George said he couldn't stay long, he had something to attend to at home."

If Shannon had left Gwen at ten past eight he should have arrived at the Country Club before eight-thirty. But he had not arrived until nine o'clock, which could mean either that he had had a very leisurely drive or that he had dashed out to Rowan Lodge to commit a very swift murder. With mixed feelings Furnival restored him to the list.

"What was Mr. Shannon's manner like?" he asked. "Did he seem normal?"

"Well, now that you mention it he was rather quiet—as though he had something on his mind. I asked him twice if anything was the matter, and he said he had had a row with his wife that morning. Not that that was anything out of the ordinary. She leads poor George an awful life."

Furnival stood up to go. "That will be all for now, Miss Lomax. I hope I shan't have to bother you again." In the doorway he stopped. "I suppose if I tried to give you some advice, you'd tell me to mind my own business?" He shot a glance kitchenwards. "No, I don't suppose you were brought up to tell your elders to mind their own business. So I'll advise you to get clear of Shannon. You're a very pretty girl, you could have your pick. Finish it off!"

Gwen looked up at him fearfully. "Is it—something to do with Miss Roach's death?"

Furnival patted her arm. "No, Gwen it's nothing to do with death. I was talking about life."

CHAPTER THIRTEEN

LAURA SHANNON sank back in her seat on the bus out of Meddenham and smiled happily. It had been a lovely day and she would be home by five o'clock, in time to get George a nice tea. Her day out had been a success right from the start. A schoolgirl neighbour had been thrilled to have the children, and the girl's mother was going to give them lunch.

Laura had deposited her offspring at ten o'clock and gone across to *Pam's Pantry* for coffee. Buying a cup of coffee only a hundred yards from her own kitchen was a way of life that appealed to Laura. Besides, Miss Wittering's cakes were altogether beyond her talents and Laura had eaten two of them before catching the eleven o'clock bus to Meddenham.

In Meddenham she had visited an old girl-friend who had given her lunch, and then she had spent a delightful afternoon looking round the shops. She had chosen a lovely green coat with a nylon fur collar, and the saving over lunch meant there was enough money left for a pair of black patent pumps that looked as if they had cost much more than they had. And, as a bonus, not a few young men had ogled her in a very satisfactory way. Yes, it had been a smashing day.

Laura tweaked open her paper carriers to reassure herself that she still liked her purchases. The coat was just as pretty a green in daylight, and the smart pumps would set off her legs beautifully. She hoped George would like them. Dear George, he wasn't so bad, thought Laura. Fancy giving her eleven pounds for a day out just because . . . Laura pulled herself up. She had a mind that was adept at skirting round unpleasant facts, but she had had to work hard on it all day to forget that George's outburst of generosity had sprung from her confession that she feared he was implicated in Aunt Grace's death. And she had feared it because he had lied about the time he had left home on Monday. And in the very affectionate scene that had followed the two detectives leaving the house George had still not explained the discrepancy.

But the niggling doubt returned now, the only thing to spoil her perfect day. That—and Iris Cantwell. Laura turned hot all over at the memory of Iris Cantwell's snub. Of course Iris had always been stuck up, everybody said that. Her father had treated her like a princess. But her attitude that morning had been really unfriendly. Laura had spotted her as soon as she entered *Pam's Pantry*. Iris always looked smart, she had such lovely clothes. That morning she had been wearing a cashmere sweater and a suede jacket, not just mock like Laura's. And she was pretty, too, in a ladylike way, with her slim figure and her smooth dark hair.

I suppose I shouldn't have spoken to her, thought Laura miserably. But on the same impulse to establish intimacy that she had felt towards Sergeant Cantwell on the previous night, she had taken a seat at Iris's table.

It was clear right away that her move had been a mistake. Iris had looked pointedly around at the several empty tables in the café, and then moved her handbag about half an inch. Miss Wittering's tables were intended for two, two chairs attended them, but they were only really adequate for delicately proportioned ladies. Laura spread her bulging handbag, her gloves, and her cigarettes over the crowded surface and beamed at Iris.

"You're Iris Cantwell, aren't you?" she said. "I've seen you about the town. I'm Laura Shannon. Your husband came to see us last night."

Iris smiled thinly. "David doesn't talk about his work at home," she said.

Laura felt rebuffed. "Well, it wasn't really work. He came to pick up a lot of old forms and stuff that were left behind when Sergeant Wainwright retired."

"Wainwright was hopelessly inefficient, I believe."

"I suppose I should have handed the things in before, but we've been awfully busy. But I'm taking a day off today. I'm going to Meddenham—to buy a new coat," said Laura airily.

Iris bit into an explosion of cream pastry with enviable aplomb. "Really?" she said.

"We've been doing up the old station house," Laura rattled on. "We've been painting and plastering and papering for months."

"Yes, it's an awful old dump, isn't it?" said Iris sweetly. "The new station flat isn't too bad for the time being, but, of course, Daddy is building us a house out at Binningdale."

Laura suddenly loved her old house fiercely. "It's going to look lovely when it's finished," she said.

"I'm so glad." Iris smiled the tight smile again, gathered

up her expensive handbag and the gloves that were as fine as a second skin and left.

Even Laura, not the most sensitive person in the world, realised that she had been snubbed. Her cheeks burning, she concentrated on her cake for a minute. When she looked up she saw Miss Wittering hovering near, glancing inquisitively at her. "Hello, Miss Wittering," she said.

"Laura, *dear*. I was so shocked to hear about poor Miss Roach, deeply shocked. For a woman to work so hard all her life only to be denied a few years of tranquillity at the end."

"Yes, it was dreadful," Laura said, stifling an impulse to reply that Aunt Grace had loathed tranquillity.

"And when is the funeral."

"Tomorrow at noon, Miss Wittering."

"Oh, dear. I would have liked to pay my last respects, but unfortunately that's my busiest time. However, I've ordered a beautiful floral tribute."

She suddenly bobbed her head down beside Laura's. "This tramp they've got in prison at Meddenham, is he the one who did it?"

"I really don't know."

Miss Wittering was disappointed. "I thought perhaps the police might have told your husband something." She lowered her voice until it was almost a nudge. "It was a terrible thing, but there'll be a bit of good for you in it, eh?"

In her effervescent morning mood it had been difficult not to giggle at Miss Wittering's conversation, but now, as she alighted from the bus in Elmbridge, Laura had to fight hard to hang on to her buoyancy. That's what everyone will be saying on the quiet, she thought. Aunt Grace had a lot of money and we were so hard up we couldn't wait for her to die. Goodness knows George and I complained often enough about being broke, but it wasn't desperate. It wasn't *that* desperate.

She let herself into the house and went through into the kitchen. She decided to make herself a cup of tea before she fetched the children and started George's meal. It would cheer her up, and besides she was suddenly rather cold. She took off her coat and put the kettle on the stove. As she set out her cup and saucer she found she was chafing her fingertips together. Why *was* she so cold? The kitchen was usually quite snug. Then a little draught on the back of her neck caused her to turn round, and she saw the neat hole that had been smashed out of the kitchen window alongside the window catch.

Sergeant Cantwell answered Laura's call in ten minutes.

"Yes, I would say you've definitely had a break-in," he announced. "It doesn't look like the work of kids. Is anything missing?"

"I don't know. I've just got back from Meddenham. I've been out all day."

"Yes, Iris told me she had seen you. Naughty girl! You knew I was going to call."

"I'm sorry. I needed to get a coat for the funeral, and George insisted that I had the day out—he gave me eleven pounds! He thought it would take my mind off things."

"He was probably right. Is this the coat?" Cantwell opened Laura's carrier bag and peeped inside. "*Very* pretty. It'll suit you."

Laura giggled. "Do you think so?"

"I certainly do. Bring out the green in your eyes. Do

you think we could have a look round to see if anything is missing?"

"Yes. But I have to fetch the children soon. Where shall we start?"

They started upstairs with the bedrooms. The rooms were all very untidy, but Laura was fairly sure that they were just as she had left them. She found herself warming to Cantwell more and more. He was so understanding when she apologised for the state of the bedrooms, appreciating that getting two small children ready and dressing herself for town had left no time for housework that morning. George was always so cutting about what he termed her slovenliness. Mr. Furnival was nice, but he was formal, this young man had a twinkle in his eye and treated her like a woman.

Cantwell on his part was dispassionately pleased with his success in loosening Laura Shannon's tongue. He was an ambitious young man. He had never been involved in an important enquiry before, but he knew by instinct that he could be a first rate detective. This could be his big chance. He thought Furnival liked him.

Laura was now leading him down the narrow dark staircase at the back of the house. The detention section of the house was quite separate from the living quarters, with its own staircase and a thick steel door smothered with bolts on both floors. Laura's high heels faltered on the stairs and Cantwell took her arm gallantly.

She was a little pink when they arrived in the passage at the foot of the stairs. She clicked on the light switch and the passage was flooded with brilliant light. There was a door at each end, one into the Shannons' quarters and the other into the old station charge room. Facing them, alongside each other, were two more steel doors with hatches cut in them and small covered peepholes.

"The cells," said Laura. "Do you want to see them?"

"Yes, I'd like to."

Laura pushed open the door of the nearest cell. It was about ten by eight feet, and painted a rather incongruous shell pink. There was a built-in base for a mattress in one corner and a wash-basin and cupboard in another. The narrow barred window was at ceiling height. A quantity of children's books and toys were scattered around.

"We thought they'd make cute bedrooms for the children when they are older," Laura explained. "Or perhaps guest-rooms. People would get a kick out of saying they had slept in a cell—" She broke off with a little shudder as a sobering thought crossed her mind.

Cantwell perched on the bunk base and swung his legs. "Not bad," he said. "Quite cosy."

"I believe Mrs. Wainwright's breakfasts were a big draw," smiled Laura. "Word got about, and drunks from miles around without bed and board would nearly fight to get in."

"I can't see Iris catering for them! What happened to the mattresses, by the way?"

"What? Oh, the council took them away. Why?"

"It crossed my mind that a prisoner might have hidden something in one, served his term and come back here looking for it. Of course prisoners should be searched, but Wainwright was capable of leaving the Crown Jewels on them!"

They left the cell block and went through the dividing door into the house.

"You see, Laura," Cantwell went on. "It's hard to

puzzle out what your visitor was looking for. Do you keep valuables in the house?"

Laura laughed shortly. "We don't keep valuables anywhere."

"It's rough when you're young and the old timers have the money. Believe me, I know!" His smile was warm and companionable. "You don't think your husband did take that figure?"

"Oh, no! I'm sure he didn't."

"Don't be shocked. It must be hard for a man not to be able to buy you all the nice things you should have."

Laura looked mollified. "I'm sure he wouldn't have stolen it, Mr. Cantwell."

"Can you think of anything an intruder might have been after?"

"I'm sorry, I can't."

"Well, if you've finished in here, let's go out to the kitchen. I detected a pot of tea that shouldn't be cold yet."

"I don't think Mrs. Shannon has any notion of what they were after," Cantwell reported to Furnival. "I got her talking very freely."

"Yes, I noticed you had quite a gift for that," Furnival said dryly.

"I'm sorry if I was too informal, sir."

"Not at all. Play it by ear. You'll find you have an instinct for the right approach if you're any good at all."

They were sitting in Cantwell's office. Cantwell had returned there from the Shannons to find Furnival and King waiting for him.

"Where was Shannon?" Furnival asked suddenly.

"He was at work. He got in just as I was leaving."

" How did he react to the break-in?"

" He was inclined to pooh-pooh it. He said a kid had probably chucked a stone through it."

" But you don't think so?"

" Looked like a break-in to me, sir."

" Well, we'll see if the fingerprint chap finds anything. He's on his way from H.Q. It's very strange indeed," Furnival mused. " It can hardly be a coincidence. But what the devil were they after? And who? Murphy is in custody, that only leaves Sid, Baer and Miss Bennett."

" *Miss Bennett*?" echoed Cantwell incredulously.

" It has to be somebody. I don't think Sid could have got into the town without being seen, and I don't see what motive Baer has now. We know all about his trouble and he has the evidence back."

" There could be someone else after those papers," said King. " Suppose Shannon had been trying a spot of fund raising on other people?"

" Yes, that's possible," agreed Furnival. " If Shannon had just started his blackmailing activities things could be coming to a head over that without it being connected in any way with Miss Roach's death. But it's the very devil to prise that sort of information out of people. What about the stuff you took away, Cantwell? Is there anything interesting in that?"

" I haven't had time to go through it all," Cantwell said, " but so far it's very minor stuff. However, there's probably more still at the Shannons, there seems to be a part missing from several of the statements. Mrs. Shannon and I didn't search really thoroughly."

" Oh, yes. You were going back there today, weren't you? Did you call?"

" I went about noon, but there wasn't anybody at home. Then at lunch my wife told me she had met Laura Shannon and she seemed to be going out for the day, so I didn't bother again. I had a lot to do and it didn't seem urgent."

" Quite. And you didn't notice the broken window?"

" I'm afraid I didn't go round to the back."

" Pity. It would have narrowed the time."

The three men were silent for a minute. Then Cantwell said, " Can we find out whether Shannon was really at work today?"

Furnival looked at him surprised. " Why? He's hardly likely to break into his own house."

" I can think of two reasons," said Cantwell. " Of course, it's a bit far fetched—"

" Go ahead, shoot," said King. " God knows, we haven't got much else."

" Well, first, for no reason at all! Suppose he felt the field was narrowing too much for comfort. We've already caught him out in that discrepancy over the time he left home on Monday. He could have set up the break-in simply to distract attention from himself."

" Hmm," said Furnival. " And secondly?"

" Secondly, he may have found some blackmail material so good that he couldn't bear to hand it over. Something really juicy about somebody well-to-do that could be money in the bank for the rest of his life."

" That one won't hold water," said King promptly. " Nobody knows what papers he has there. He could extract anything he liked and no one would be any the wiser."

" Wainwright would know," said Cantwell. " His memory is marvellous and I said in front of the Shannons that I was going to get him to go through the papers with me. This way anything that was missing could be explained by the break-in."

"It's possible," said Furnival. "It's the sort of crazy solution that could make sense."

"How about me searching the Shannons' place with a warrant to see what else is there?" asked Cantwell.

"No, I don't think so," said Furnival slowly. "If there *is* something there it may act as a catalyst to set things moving. In the meantime we can certainly find out whether Shannon was in his office this afternoon."

"What about Monday night?" Cantwell asked. "Did his girl-friend alibi him for the missing hour?"

"Well, most of it."

"She could be lying."

"I don't think so. But it's immaterial because he left her early enough to dash back here and do a swift job on his aunt. According to Gwen Lomax, Shannon was quiet and tense and he left her unexpectedly early."

"And listen, Laura Shannon told me her husband insisted on her going out today," Cantwell put in eagerly. "Those were her very words. He even pressed money on her! He wanted her out of the way."

Furnival smiled at the younger man's enthusiasm. "All right, we'll look into his movements. But I'm still keeping Murphy inside. He's quite comfortable where he is, and we'll have the public down on us like a ton of bricks if we let him go."

"What about Miss Bennett?" enquired King. "Don't forget, a lot of your most notorious murders are committed by gentle middle-aged ladies!"

"She's still in," said Furnival. "Unless she spent the whole day sitting with the vicar, she's still in!"

CHAPTER FOURTEEN

THE FOLLOWING morning Furnival got to his office early. He had a meeting scheduled with Superintendent Peters and the Chief Constable to which he was not looking forward, and he intended to attend Miss Roach's funeral at noon. But first he had several instructions to relay and the Roach file to bring up to date.

He was about half-way through his chores when King arrived. King took off his jacket, lit a cigarette and settled down at his desk.

" Well, have you any rabbits to pull out of the hat?" he asked agreeably. " Just in time to save our bacon?"

"Not a sausage," said Furnival gloomily. " I've just spoken to someone at Shannon's office and they say he was out in his car most of yesterday afternoon. I called on Mrs. Milton last night, Miss Bennett was in Elmbridge all yesterday morning, collecting some more of her things from Rowan Lodge. Why are people so bloody mobile! Baer was in Elmbridge as usual, of course, and could have nipped up to the Shannons any time."

" Laura Shannon has an alibi," said King helpfully.

" She could have broken the window before she left for

Meddenham. But no, I never suspected her anyway. I don't believe she would have left her babies alone to go out to her aunt's house on Monday night. It would have taken her some time on foot. She moans about her lot, but I think she would be conscientious about her children."

"She could be in it with her husband."

"She could be, but I don't think she is. However, I do think she's scared sick that he did it. She's probably just realised how little they really know each other."

The two men worked in silence for the next hour until Furnival stood up stretching his legs.

"Well, this is it, King. We'll know better where we stand after this."

The Chief Constable had already arrived in Peters' office when Furnival got there. He was standing looking out of the window with his back to the room. He turned when Furnival entered.

Lindsay Daneman was in his forties, dark, very big, and very handsome. His beautifully cut tweed suit had been tailored a long way from Meddenham. The aroma of his expensive cigar put Furnival in mind of the Elmbridge Country Club.

"You know Chief Inspector Furnival?" Peters asked.

Daneman nodded. "We've met." He moved across to Peters' desk, and sprawled as elegantly as he could in the standard issue chair. "Not a lot of progress, Furnival," he said.

"It's a puzzling case, sir."

"And you're not puzzling it too successfully. Superintendent Peters has just been telling me about the break-in at the nephew's house. What do you make of that?"

Furnival ran through the possibilities he had considered

with King and Cantwell the previous evening. They sounded even thinner now.

"It was quite deplorable of ex-Sergeant Wainwright to leave that stuff about in the old station," said Daneman. "It was an open invitation to blackmail. Can't he be reprimanded in any way?"

"Well, he is retired now, of course," said Peters. "Perhaps a stiff letter? We don't want it to leak out if we can help it, it puts us in a very bad light."

"Yes. This chap Cantwell sounds a considerable improvement."

"He's working most reliably," said Furnival.

"You want to keep Murphy a bit longer?" Daneman asked.

"Yes, I think so. I don't see any difficulties over that."

"O.K. What about Shannon?"

"I couldn't possibly make a charge stick at the moment. It's true that he needed money, he tried that jiggery-pokery with Baer over the figure, he hasn't a good alibi for the murder or the break-in, but it's all circumstantial. We haven't a shred of evidence against him."

"No help from the Lab?"

"Nothing. But I don't think Shannon will bolt. He's a man who would like a position in the community."

"Yes, I believe I've seen the fellow at the club," Daneman said.

"The Elmbridge Country Club? Yes, he is a member. Pretty high-class place, isn't it?" Furnival asked.

"It has pretentions, but it's a bit provincial," Daneman said tolerantly. "However it's certainly not cheap. I would have thought it was a bit beyond his means."

"Sergeant Cantwell is a member, too," put in Peters.

"But he has well-heeled in-laws who like him to move in the right circles."

"Really?" Daneman watched a smoke ring drift off from his cigar. "I wouldn't have expected to run into one of my sergeants there." He did not look too pleased at the notion.

"And Baer," added Furnival. "Baer the antique dealer is a member."

"Oh, well, of course, Baer has money," Daneman said. "I know him very well. Charming fellow, perfect gentleman."

"Could he have been involved in the Coverdale Hall job?" Furnival asked.

"Only unwittingly. He has never been found to have any criminal associates either before or since. I should say he built up his business by smart practice and hard work, and only stumbled into that trouble through inexperience. However, although it's a very long shot, we mustn't overlook the possibility of some sort of connection with the Coverdale Hall affair."

"Haven't we got some other ancient crime?" asked Peters. "Wasn't the old woman attacked and robbed once before?"

"Yes, a run-of-the-mill small shop hold-up," said Furnival. "Not enough was taken to found anybody's fortune."

"It couldn't have been the nephew?"

"*Shannon*? But how? She would have recognised him."

"Did she get a look at the chap?"

"I don't know. I never enquired. But in any case Shannon was supposed to be living in London at the time."

"Shannon has a way of not actually being where he was supposed to be!" Daneman put out his cigar and studied his handsome hand-made brogues. "The point now is, do we call in the Yard, Furnival? You've had more than four days, they'll complain the case is cold now."

Furnival hesitated. "I'd like a bit longer, but I can't claim that I'm on the verge of a breakthrough."

"If I gave you until Monday morning do you think you could do anything useful with the time?"

Furnival still hesitated. "I couldn't promise any solid results."

"Cautious blighter, aren't you? O.K., you've got it anyway. Until first thing Monday morning. Then I'll contact the Yard and let their wrath fall about my head."

"Thank you, sir."

"Is there anything you want me to do? What about this mental lad, what's-his-name—Robbins? You aren't forgetting him, are you?"

"No, sir. I'm not forgetting him."

"Well, why hasn't he turned up? He can't be all that self-reliant. Do you think he's in the river?"

"I think it's possible. He could have fallen in, jumped in, or, if he saw something he shouldn't, been chucked in."

"Do you want to start dragging? Perhaps the stretch from the town to Rowan Lodge to begin with."

"I think it would be advisable, sir."

"Right!" Daneman flicked through the pages of the case file and handed it back to Furnival. "It's your baby. Keep me in touch with any developments. Good luck, Furnival!"

Furnival returned to his office.

"How was the Great Profile?" asked King.

"Still posing for *Town and Country*. No, to be honest, he was very fair."

He recounted what had happened in Peters's office, leaving King with mixed feelings about still 'going it alone', then put on a raincoat and started out in torrential rain for Miss Roach's funeral.

The funeral was to be held in Meddenham cemetery, the small churchyard at Elmbridge having filled to capacity many years ago. Furnival spotted the crowd from the gate and hurried towards it. There was a fair turn-out considering the weather, and several heads turned to look curiously at him as he joined the group. He got the impression that the bulk of the crowd were the usual ghouls attracted by the murder rather than mourners. They did not look like acquaintances Miss Roach would have encouraged. The only faces he recognised were those of Shannon, and Miss Bennett, looking shockingly ill and supported by her sister. The service had just begun and the parson rattled through it in a perfunctory manner stopping once or twice to wipe the rain from his glasses. When it was over George Shannon was the first away, avoiding Furnival's eye as he scuttled for his car. Miss Bennett and Mrs. Milton, arm-in-arm, passed close to him, Miss Bennett nodding nervously, her sister graciously. The rest of the crowd dispersed slowly. Furnival realised he was very wet and very hungry, hurried to his car and drove home.

He found Joanna with her feet up in the lounge reading a library book.

"A woman's work is never done," he remarked. "Any chance of something to eat?"

Joanna lowered her feet and stared at the clock. "At one o'clock?" she asked with elaborate sarcasm. "Watch it, darling, you're turning into a normal husband. And don't drip on the carpet."

Furnival hung his coat over a chair in the kitchen and towelled his hair while Joanna put a couple of chops under the grill.

"I suppose you're going out again as soon as you've eaten?" she said.

"Yes, I must be at Elmbridge. They're going to drag the river."

Joanna said nothing. She knew this was an activity her husband loathed. She set the table, and when the food was ready put it in front of him."

"Aren't you having anything?" he asked.

"I had mine just before you came in. Shall I get you some coffee?"

"Please." Furnival ate the hot food and watched the rain tumble past the window of the bright kitchen. He thought of Sid Robbins, cold and hungry and alone on the desolate moor.

Joanna made the coffee and sat down close to Furnival. She poured out two cups.

"He must have found shelter somewhere," she said.

"Where? He hadn't anywhere to go except his home and Rowan Lodge, or out on the moor. There's just nowhere he could make for—" He broke off.

"What is it?" asked Joanna.

"Just a thought, a slim chance. I should have thought of it before." He stood up, pushing back his chair. "It depends how far away it is."

"But where?" Joanna called. Furnival was making for the telephone in the hall.

"He was at a residential school, until he was fifteen. His doctor said to me, 'He was very happy there.' I shouldn't have overlooked it."

"But they wouldn't let him stay. They would contact you. There's been plenty about him in the papers."

"He could be hiding out. It's half-term holiday, there may be no one there. Of course, it could be at the other end of England." He dialled a number and heard Dr. Swinney's voice. They spoke for a few minutes, then Furnival put down the receiver and looked at Joanna. "Hunnington House. It's seventeen miles across the moor. He could have made it."

Furnival's first act was to telephone the school. There was no reply. Then he telephoned Peters and asked for the dragging of the river to be held up until he had searched the school.

"It sounds worth looking into," the Superintendent said. "But let us know what happens as soon as you can. It's no use starting to drag when it's getting dark. Who are you taking with you?"

"I'll pick up King and get a couple of blokes from Elmbridge."

"O.K. We've got a man at Hunnington. Contact him first. Good luck!"

Furnival gulped down a cup of coffee, kissed Joanna, and ran out to his car. He felt that there was a real chance of some action at last. At H.Q. he waited impatiently for King to finish his canteen cottage pie, and they headed once more for Elmbridge.

Cantwell was waiting for them on the steps of the station. "What's happened? We were waiting for your chaps to arrive to make a start on the river, but Superintendent Peters has just rung to say that it's off. Have you got Robbins?"

Furnival explained about the school. "It seems worth

taking a look before we start dragging the river. It's a hell of a job, and not pleasant for the local people. Can you spare a couple of men to come over to Hunnington?"

"I'll come myself, and Sperry is available. He knows the country well."

"Fine. He's a good man." They hastily collected Sperry and a second car. "You lead and we'll follow," said Furnival. "You know the way, Sperry?"

"Yes, sir, it's about twenty-four miles."

"Dr. Swinney said seventeen."

"That would be direct across the moors, sir. We can't take the cars that way."

"Well, as fast as you can."

The two cars drove out of Elmbridge over the bridge. Through the steamy windows. Furnival could see the river, fast and turbulent, churning around the buttresses of the bridge, and he hoped fervently that their excursion would not be in vain. They passed the drive of Rowan Lodge and the turn for Shalebeach. Just as the *Black Cat* transport café came into sight a faint watery sun broke through the cloud.

CHAPTER FIFTEEN

About three miles past the transport café the cars turned off into a secondary road which immediately began to wind steeply uphill. Furnival looked out of the window and saw that the country had taken on a moorland character. They passed two or three small hamlets, but mostly there were only isolated farmhouses, gaunt and inhospitable against the bleak landscape. When they had gone twenty miles Sperry turned off again into a side road. Below them a fast flowing tributary of the Elm ran parallel with the road.

After a mile or two the scattered outskirts of Hunnington began to appear, a farm, a huddle of houses, a chapel, then standing on its own, the police house. Cantwell and Sperry got out of the leading car and waited for Furnival. As Furnival stopped his car the local constable came out of the house and looked at them in bewilderment. He was a fat and comfortable man in his fifties. He wore a pair of ancient corduroy trousers and a woollen shirt, and he looked sleepy. Disturbed his afternoon sport on the telly, Furnival thought. The man brought Sergeant Wainwright to his mind, a man he had heard plenty about but never met.

He went up the path to meet the local man, introduced

himself and the others, and briefly explained their business. The man, whose name was Wordsworth, invited them into his very warm front room and switched off the television set which had been showing a football match.

"I did hear about the boy being missing," he said, "but I reckoned this was too far for him to get. Of course, I didn't know about him going to school here."

"I should have thought of this place before now," Furnival said. "Is the school closed?"

"Yes, sir, they've got a week's holiday. There won't be anybody there, leastwise only Bill Kennedy. He's the caretaker and gardener, he's got a room at the House."

"Wouldn't he have spotted Robbins if he'd turned up?" asked Cantwell.

"Not necessarily. Old Kennedy is getting on a bit, and it's a big rambling house, as you'll see."

"How many children are there at the school?" Furnival asked.

"Only about thirty. They like to keep the numbers down to keep it homey."

"How do the local people take to them? Are they allowed into the town?" asked King.

Wordsworth looked at him in surprise. "Well, of course they're allowed into the town. They're only backward kiddies, you know, not loonies. Country people understand about some folk being a bit different." He struggled into an old tweed overcoat looking faintly huffy.

This is the right place for Sid, Furnival thought. "We don't want him to see the cars if he should be watching," he said. "Is it far to walk from here?"

"I understand. You want to creep up on him, like? No, it's not far. Less than a mile."

He added a cap to his ensemble, and, opening the door, yelled towards the rear of the house, "I'm off out, Ma! Police business!"

The five men left the house and started through Hunnington. It was a small town, barely worthy of the title, just half a dozen streets round a central square, a pub, a chapel, and a tiny cinema now given over to bingo. It was hard to see why a town had grown up in such a place. They struck straight across the centre and took a road leading out of town on the far side. When they had followed it for about three hundred yards they saw just ahead of them four very large detached houses, set in big gardens, and with a dense mass of trees and shrubbery masking their gates. As they passed the first of these Wordsworth said, "The last of these big houses is the school."

Furnival stopped and looked ahead. He could see a frontage of about a hundred yards of dark trees and halfway along it a break where the gate must be. Nothing of the house was visible.

The men got into the side of the road and walked quietly in single file beneath the trees. At the drive they stopped. There was an iron gate across it, and just beyond that, a large signboard which read *Hunnington House. Residential School.*

Furnival opened the gate and the men slipped through. They took to the cover of the dense shrubbery as far as it extended. Where it ended at the edge of the lawn Furnival stopped them again, and still in the cover of the trees they regarded the house.

Nobody could ever have called Hunnington House beautiful, still less homely. It was a large and ugly Victorian Gothic edifice, its dark slate purplish after the rain. It had steep twin gables, a couple of superfluous towers stuck on at the corners, and a great deal of stained glass.

"Blimey! What a grim looking place," King exclaimed. "Bleak House! What was it originally? A workhouse?"

"It was a very posh prep school," Wordsworth explained. "The upper classes don't object to tough conditions for their kids. Particularly if they're paying a lot for it."

Furnival looked at the house with disappointment. "No one would run to this place," he said.

"It's not so bad inside," Wordsworth said loyally. "What can you do with a building like that?"

"Well, we'd better take a look now we're here," said Furnival. "But I don't want the lot of us marching across the lawn. Is there any way we can get nearer the house under cover?"

"We can work our way round to the back, that way we won't be so exposed."

"Right. You lead the way, Wordsworth. Where is this chap Kennedy likely to be? There was no answer when I telephoned."

"He could be anywhere. There are several outbuildings." They followed Wordsworth in silence, working their way round the house through the shrubbery. The undergrowth was sodden beneath their feet, and every movement released a deluge of rain on to their heads from the foliage above. Along the west side of the house was a long new prefabricated building.

"Crafts and hobbies building," Wordsworth whispered. "They do a lot of that."

As the back of the house came into view Furnival saw that an effort had been made to make it look attractive. The walls up to the first floor had been painted pink and tubs of flowers stood about. There was a well-equipped playground with swings and a climbing frame, and in the branches of a big tree a tree house had been built with a rope ladder dangling to the ground. A long greenhouse stretched almost from the house to where they stood.

"All right," said Furnival. "We'll close in from here."

They edged along the side of the greenhouse to the cover of the house, then hugged the wall of the house until they reached the back porch. The elaborate caution seemed to Furnival faintly ridiculous in a place that appeared to be completely deserted. He rang the bell on the porch. It pealed stridently through the house for some moments, but there was no response. They had just opened the door and stepped inside the back hall when a man appeared hurrying down a staircase at the end of a passage.

"I'm coming. I'm coming," he called. "I was right at the top of the house." He came up to the policemen, puffing slightly, a small puckish man in his sixties, with a very brown face and a few tufts of reddish-brown hair. "What is it you want?"

"This is Chief Inspector Furnival from Meddenham," Wordsworth explained. "He's looking for one of your lads who has gone missing."

"A young man by the name of Sid Robbins," Furnival said. "You may not remember him, he would have left here some years ago."

"I remember Sid Robbins well," Kennedy said. "He was one of the nicest lads we ever had here. But surely he's not in trouble with the police?"

"He's wanted in connection with a murder enquiry at Elmbridge," Furnival said. "His employer was found murdered and Robbins has been missing for five days. Naturally I want to interview him. You must have heard the hue-and-cry?"

"I'm very quiet here in the holidays. I don't get to hear anything. But I can tell you, sir, young Sid would never hurt anyone. He used to help me about the place and I got to know him really well. If anything happened to upset him he'd run off and hide, that was his way. He wouldn't hurt a fly."

"Nevertheless, we have to find him. He may have witnessed something. Could he be hiding somewhere here?"

"No, sir, no chance. I would have spotted him. In any case he would have needed food by this time."

"Do you mind if we have a look around?"

Kennedy shrugged. "Please yourself." He led the policemen up the back staircase to the top floor of the house where they split up, Furnival and Cantwell taking the top floor, King and Sperry the second, with Wordsworth dogging their heels. Both the top floors were entirely given over to dormitories and bathrooms. The bedrooms were bright and attractively furnished, with only four beds to a room. Furnival and Cantwell got down to the first floor just as King and Sperry arrived. King shook his head to indicate that they too had found nothing. The first floor housed a comfortable day-room, a games room, and the staff sitting-room and bedrooms, and down on the ground floor was the dining-room, cloakrooms, and offices. It was a big rambling house, with two staircases and innumerable cupboards, lavatories, and storerooms, and it was over an hour before Furnival was reasonably satisfied that Robbins was nowhere on the premises. The detectives reassembled in Kennedy's tiny cubby-hole beside the back door. An armchair was pulled up before a gas fire; an empty tea cup, a newspaper and a pair of spectacles lay to hand on a table.

"This is a very pleasant place for the children," Furnival said.

"It's their home," said Kennedy simply. "Some of them break their hearts when they have to leave."

"Did Sid Robbins?"

"Yes, he took it very hard. Take my word for it, sir. Sid would never do anything vicious."

Cantwell who had been standing beside the table, suddenly opened Kennedy's newspaper and spread it out.

"Don't you read the headlines, Mr. Kennedy?" he asked.

Furnival looked at the paper. Even from where he stood he could see the Roach case headlined in black type and the photograph of Sid Robbins. He turned back to the caretaker.

"Why did you pretend to know nothing of the murder?" he asked.

"I never noticed it, sir. I was reading the racing. I only read the sport pages. Why would I lie to you? You've seen Sid isn't here."

"We'll look over the outbuildings," Furnival said.

"Certainly, sir." Kennedy bustled them towards the back door. "I'll get the keys."

As they reached the back door Furnival noticed, just beyond it, a narrow flight of stairs leading down into the basement. "What's down there?" he asked.

"Just stores, sir. The cokestore and the cleaning stuffs." Kennedy held the back door open.

Furnival ignored it. "We'll go down there."

Kennedy scuttled ahead of them like an eager crab.

"There couldn't be anyone down there. Everything is locked up when the school is empty. There's no way in."

The five men clattered on down the stone staircase past Kennedy. At the foot was a short passage with four doors leading off it.

"Unlock the doors," Furnival said.

Kennedy unlocked the two nearest doors and they looked into large store cupboards. King pushed inside and looked around, lifting aside the cartons that were piled high against the walls.

"Nothing," he said as he came out.

At the third door Kennedy hesitated. Furnival reached out and tried the handle. The door opened to reveal a much larger cupboard, almost a small room. It seemed to contain stationery and school equipment, but none of the men was looking at the shelves. On the floor in front of them a rough bed had been made up with blankets and pillows. A mug and a plate with the remains of a meal stood beside the bed, and on a nearby shelf was a well-thumbed stack of children's comics.

Furnival turned on the caretaker. "Where is he, Kennedy? You knew he was here. You've been hiding him."

As the man opened his mouth to speak they heard a faint crunching sound. "Listen!" Cantwell shouted. The noise came again, louder this time, and he pushed through the other men and wrenched open the last door in the corridor. In the gloom they could see it was a large coke cellar with a huge pile of coke reaching almost to the ceiling. Just above the crest of the pile was a metal grating leading outside. The grill had been lifted aside and through the aperture a leg was disappearing.

"There he goes!" Cantwell shouted. He started to run up the pile of coke, but slithered back to the floor.

"Outside," King yelled. He grabbed Kennedy by the shoulder. "Where does this place come out?"

"Near the corner of the house," Kennedy gasped. "Opposite the greenhouse. But listen. sir, don't hurt him! Please don't hurt him!"

They left him babbling and dashed for the stairs. Furnival and Cantwell found themselves outside first, the older men behind them. Furnival quickly scanned the trees beyond the lawn.

"Over there!" he said, as a figure slipped into the shrubbery.

They pounded across to where Robbins had disappeared. There was no sign of him. Furnival gripped Cantwell's shoulder and they froze into silence. Immediately they heard, not far ahead of them, the sound of heavy feet breaking through the undergrowth. They started in the direction of the noise, and after some fifty yards came to a shoulder high stone wall. They vaulted the wall and dropped into a paddock on the other side. Robbins was haring across open country about thirty yards ahead of them.

"Stop!" Furnival shouted. "Stop Sid! We just want to talk to you."

The lanky figure wavered for a moment, looking back over his shoulder.

Furnival advanced slowly towards him as though stalking a nervous horse. "Come on, Sid, let's have a chat. Then we'll take you home to your mother. She's very worried about you."

Robbins looked from one to the other of them. He took

a few stumbling steps backwards, then turned round and was off again.

"Damn!" Furnival muttered. "I thought he was coming."

"He can't get much further," Cantwell panted. "The river!"

Furnival looked. Just ahead of Sid the river flowed in a deep cut channel, hard to see from a distance. It was not wide, but fast flowing. It was impossible to judge its depth.

Sid Robbins had already reached the river. He looked at the rapidly advancing policemen for a moment, an expression of desperation on his face, then he plunged in.

The water reached his chest, and he floundered for a moment, arms flailing, before he regained his balance and started to wade slowly forward. He was almost at the farther bank when Cantwell with a burst of speed reached the water. He had slipped out of his jacket as he ran, and he jumped straight into the water and advanced on the wading youth in a swift powerful crawl. Robbins looked back, his face blank with terror, then he tried to scramble up the opposite bank, his fingers slipping and sliding in the steep muddy walls. As he fell back for the third time Cantwell grabbed him round the waist and the two men disappeared together beneath the water. Furnival hesitated on the water's edge, but Cantwell very obviously needed no assistance. As Sid surfaced, gasping and spluttering, Cantwell splayed his hand over his face and pushed it below the water again. Then he wrenched Robbins round and pinned his arms behind his back. The young sergeant's temper seemed to match his hair. He would be a useful man to have beside you in a scrap down in Meddenham dock on a Saturday night, Furnival thought, but under these circumstances he was somewhat overdoing the violence.

"O.K., that's enough, Cantwell!" he shouted. "You're drowning the poor devil." He held out his hand and helped the two men from the water. Robbins offered no resistance, but sank down gasping and choking on the bank. King, Sperry and Wordsworth came up to join them. Kennedy walked through the group, ignoring the policemen. He knelt down beside Robbins and taking off his jacket put it round his shoulders.

"Come back to the house, Sid," he said. "Bill will look after you."

The youth looked up at the old man and clutched at him like a child. "Don't send me back to her," he said. "She'll shout at me and hit me with her stick like she did to Miss Bennett. I didn't do anything wrong. Please don't send me back!"

CHAPTER SIXTEEN

IT WAS more than two hours before Furnival got Sid Robbins back to Elmbridge. They had first taken him to Hunnington House where Kennedy had found dry clothes for him and Cantwell, and made hot drinks for the two soaked and shivering men. Wordsworth was dismissed and returned home after the biggest excitement in his entire career.

Gradually Robbins' distraught state had quietened down, and after lengthy reassurances from Kennedy, he had got into the police car, sitting meekly between Furnival and Kennedy. They had taken him directly to the Elmbridge station, while Cantwell and Sperry stopped on the way to pick up Mrs. Robbins.

Sid sat gauche and awkward in the office chair, looking more excited now than frightened. His mother sat very close to him, a dirty raincoat over her apron, pressing pieces of chocolate on her son from a large bar she had managed to procure on the way. Mrs. Robbins was a mother who believed that all her children's problems could be assuaged by stuffing sweetmeats into their mouths.

Furnival began very gently with Sid. "We're very glad

you've turned up safely, Sid. We were all worried about you."

Sid grinned amiably. The chocolate coated his teeth thickly. "Mr. Kennedy looked after me," he said.

"Yes, you had a nice holiday, didn't you? Have you been back to visit Mr. Kennedy before, since you left school?"

Sid looked vague. "I tried to go on the bus three or four times, but sometimes the bus went to the wrong place and I had to walk home. But once I really got there, and Mr. Kennedy gave me a lovely tea." Sid smiled happily at the memory. "Lots of cake."

"Lovely. But this time you walked all the way?"

"Got no money for the bus. It was a long walk."

"It certainly was. How did you manage to find the school. Did you go across the moor?"

Again Sid looked blank.

"How did you know how to get to Mr. Kennedy?" Furnival persisted. "How did you find him?"

The boy's face cleared. "I went the way the bus goes."

"Along the road? A lot of cars passed you?"

"Yes, whoosh, whoosh. all the time. Nearly knocked me down."

"But you got there. Clever lad. Why did you go, Sid?"

"I wanted to see Mr. Kennedy."

"But why then particularly? After dinner on Monday. You were supposed to go back to work, you know."

Sid's face clouded over. "He don't have no sense of time, sir," Mrs. Robbins interrupted. "Last Monday won't mean anything to him." She turned to her son. "You was a bad lad, Sid. You come in and didn't say a word to me and the kids. You was too early for your dinner. What did you do with that nice bacon sandwich I made you? Did you eat it up?"

Sid thought deeply. His eyes ranged over the ring of faces watching him so closely. "Ate it when I got back to work," he said finally.

"You mustn't tell fibs, you naughty boy. You know you didn't go back to work."

"Just a minute, Mrs. Robbins," Furnival murmured. "Where did you eat your sandwich, Sid?"

"In the garden shed at the bottom of the garden."

"And then what did you do?"

"I went on with my work. I sawed logs and chopped the firewood, and swept up the leaves for a bonfire like Miss Bennett had said, and then I mended my barrow."

"All this was away from the house?"

"Yes, sir."

"So you didn't see either Miss Roach or Miss Bennett in the afternoon?"

"No." Sid looked uncomfortable. "Miss Roach was angry. She was shouting. I didn't break the little china man."

"I'm sure you didn't. Do you know what happened to it?"

Sid pondered again. "I seen a man in our lane. Miss Bennett seen him, too. Perhaps he took it. Miss Roach sent for the policeman on the telephone." Sid pointed at Cantwell. "That policeman. We told him about the man."

"Well, why did you run away? Miss Roach didn't blame you, did she? What made you decide to go to Hunnington?"

For the first time Robbins looked sullen and stubborn. He stared at his huge hands knotting between his knees. "I didn't like her shouting. I didn't like the policeman coming."

"Sergeant Cantwell didn't frighten you, did he?"

Sid shook his head. "Well, what made you take off?" Furnival tried another line. "What time did you go?"

"When it was time to go home."

Furnival glanced at Mrs. Robbins. "He's supposed to leave at six o'clock," she said.

"So you spent the whole afternoon at Rowan Lodge and no one saw you? And you didn't see Miss Roach or Miss Bennett? Didn't you go up to the house before you left?"

There was the longest pause yet. Sid stared at his hands. Furnival could hear the breathing of all the people in the room.

"Come on, Sid," he coaxed gently. "We're not going to hurt you. I know you didn't do anything wrong."

"Speak up, Sid," Kennedy urged. "Tell them what you know, lad."

Sid's eyes came up and met Kennedy's as though drawing strength from him. "They was fighting," he whispered.

"Who was fighting?" Furnival's voice was as low as Sid's.

"Miss Roach and Miss Bennett. I went up to the house to change my shoes. I heard Miss Roach shouting. I looked through the window. She was screaming at Miss Bennett and she had her walking stick up like this—" Sid raised one arm above his head, "as though she was going to hit her. I was frightened and I ran away. I thought she would hit me. I started to walk to Mr. Kennedy, I was crying because I couldn't stop her hitting Miss Bennett who was always nice to me. But I was frightened."

Furnival turned to Kennedy. "What time did Sid arive at Hunnington?" he asked.

"At half-past-twelve. He didn't sneak in. He just hung on the doorbell until I got out of bed and went down to answer it."

"What did he say?"

"He didn't make much sense, but he was cold and exhausted so I took him in. I knew it would all come out gradually. It's happened before with other lads. They haven't done anything against the law; it's just that the world is too much for them for a few days, so they come back to me."

"When did you know we were looking for Robbins?" King asked.

"Not until Thursday morning. Then I got him out of the dormitory and down into the basement in case you should think of coming to the school for him. I knew he hadn't killed that old woman and I thought he would be better out of the way until all the unpleasantness was cleared up. I was going to contact you soon, anyway. The kids are due back on Tuesday."

"Half-past-twelve," mused Furnival. "And he walked twenty-four miles, well, twenty-three from Rowan Lodge. Did you take any rests, Sid?"

"I sat in the hedge twice, sir, just for a few minutes."

"You didn't get a lift in a car?"

"No, sir."

"Did you walk quickly?"

"As quick as I could."

"This fight between Miss Roach and Miss Bennett," put in King. "Can you remember anything that was said? I mean, what were they shouting about?"

Sid screwed up his brow in an effort at remembrance. "Miss Roach was saying Miss Bennett was careless and—and stupid. She said she was more trouble than she was worth, and she was so careless she'd better go."

"You didn't see Miss Bennett hit back in any way?"

"Oh, no, sir, she just crouched herself up and cried."

"Miss Roach wasn't a bad woman," Mrs. Robbins said. "She was hard, but then she'd had a hard life. She was a good, just woman in her way. Something must have really upset her to go for Miss Bennett like that."

"Well, we'll find out about that," Furnival said. "Just one more question, Sid. Did you see anybody hanging around Rowan Lodge on Monday afternoon, while you were doing your work, or when you were running away to Mr. Kennedy? Think carefully."

Furnival pressed the boy on the point for as long as he dared, but Sid could recall seeing no strangers apart from Murphy on Sunday.

The statements from Sid and Bill Kennedy were finally completed and signed. Mrs. Robbins and Kennedy were returned home, and Sid was taken to the cottage hospital for the night. There a doctor could check him over, and a discreet watch could be kept on him. It seemed to Furnival that he was in no emotional state to go home yet, but to have locked him up in a cell could have done him untold harm.

"Apart from which he may well be guilty," said Cantwell. The Elmbridge sergeant, dressed in the strange assortment of clothes Kennedy had found for him, for the first time looked dispirited.

"Not if he walked all the way." Furnival gathered up the papers from the desk and packed them into his briefcase. " He was at Hunnington, twenty-three miles away, by twelve-thirty, *and* he took a couple of rests. He must have left Rowan Lodge by six o'clock at the latest, even so he would have had to keep up nearly four miles an hour for six hours."

" Tough going," said King. " It would be dark more than half the way."

" Maybe he did get a lift," said Cantwell.

" It's not impossible, although the driver should have reported it by this time. It's a murder case, and we've had plenty of appeals out. I thought Sid's story rang true."

" Maybe Miss Bennett started to fight back after Robbins had left," suggested Cantwell.

" Then they would have had to fight for an hour if the pathologist is right and Miss Roach didn't die before seven o'clock. In any case, Miss Roach did not die fighting, she died sitting peacefully in her chair."

" We'd better ring the Super," King said.

" What can I tell him? The case is closed?"

" You can tell him there's no need to drag the river," Cantwell said helpfully.

" True. And I can tell him that the Meissen figure can be dismissed from the case because in all probability Miss Bennett broke it while she was dusting. But if I know the Super he'll regard those as somewhat negative statements. What the Super will want to know, my dear Cantwell, is who-dun-it?"

" I'm damned if I can make any sense of it." Cantwell scratched his flaming mop. " It's all so unrelated."

" Well, it's no use conjecturing in limbo," said Furnival. He glanced out of the window and was surprised to see that it was quite dark. He looked at his watch. It was nearly nine o'clock. " Let's go and see if we can scare some truth out of Miss Bennett, and I hope to God Mrs. Milton is out dominating a bingo club somewhere!"

" I'll come with you," Cantwell said.

" No, you're home now, stay here," said Furnival seriously. " You've had a heavy week and you need some rest. You're not doing the Force any good working yourself into the ground."

He left with King for Meddenham and, as he had hoped, found Miss Bennett alone in her sister's flat. When the housekeeper opened the door to the detectives, after first peeping round it like a timid mouse, she backed half-way into the room, her eyes frantically darting to right and left as though seeking the support of her absent sister.

" I'm sorry to trouble you so late. I'll only keep you a few minutes." Furnival said, " First, perhaps you'd like to know that Sid has turned up."

" Oh, I'm so glad. I've been worried about him," Miss Bennett looked genuinely pleased. " Is he all right?"

" He appears to be perfectly all right. He was at a residential school he once attended."

" At Hunnington? How silly of me! I should have suggested you looked there. Sid used to talk such a lot about it. It was thoughtful of you to let me know he was safe, Mr. Furnival."

" That isn't quite all, Miss Bennett. May we sit down?"

When they were settled in the cosy cluttered living-room, Furnival said, " Sid Robbins made a statement. It seems he didn't run off at lunch-time as we thought. He says he returned to Rowan Lodge and worked there all afternoon away from the house. Is that possible?"

"Oh, yes, Sid is a good worker. He doesn't have to be watched."

"He says that he didn't actually leave until about six o'clock."

Miss Bennett still showed no perturbation, only mild curiosity. "He usually leaves about six."

"He also said that he went up to the house just before he left and overheard a violent quarrel between you and Miss Roach."

Miss Bennett's tenuous self-control left her. Her weak face crumpled. "That Sid!" she whispered. "He exaggerates so. The least thing upsets him."

"Miss Roach wasn't shouting at you?"

"I expect so," she managed a bitter laugh. "When wasn't she? I remember it was something about—yes, about not sweeping the leaves from the back hall. They will blow in, and I'd forgotten to sweep them out. But I *told* you, Mr. Furnival, I told you when you called before, that Miss Roach had said horrid things to me and made me cry."

"I know you did. But I hadn't realised it was quite so violent—Sid said that Miss Roach had her stick raised."

"Oh, no, I don't think she did anything like that. In any case, you're talking about what Miss Roach was doing to *me*. I wouldn't do anything to her. I'm a servant, Mr. Furnival. My sister doesn't like me to say it, but I am. If I wasn't a servant to Miss Roach I would be to somebody else. That's the sort of person I am." She stopped and tried to hold her mouth firm. Furnival looked at King who shrugged helplessly.

"Miss Bennett," Furnival said. "Don't you think we could have an end to this fiction? The row was nothing to do with clearing leaves, was it? Sid said he heard Miss

Roach shouting that you were careless. That doesn't sound to me as though it had anything to do with skimping the chores. Slovenly, lazy, perhaps. Not careless."

"Sid doesn't choose his words exactly."

"He wasn't choosing words, he was quoting. Miss Roach may have scolded you about the leaves on other occasions, but if she was mad that day I think it was about her china figure." Furnival scowled at Miss Bennett's wretched face in exasperation. "Oh, come on! All I want is to get the bloody thing eliminated from the case once and for all!"

It had its effect. Miss Bennett gave a little spluttering moan, and tears started to pour down her face. She made one or two abortive attempts at speech, but it took five minutes, and much comforting patting of her back from King, before she was anything like articulate.

"I daren't own up," she choked. "It was so pretty and so precious. I'd broken things before and she'd been furiously angry. And this was her dearest possession. I was terrified she'd sack me. But after Mr. Cantwell came out to the house and questioned everybody and started looking for the tramp, I knew I had to own up before I caused any more trouble. So after tea I plucked up courage and confessed. It was terrible, I'd never seen her so angry. She did raise her stick at me. I think it was as much for making her look a fool as breaking the fiddler. The rest of what I told you was true. I went to my room and bathed my face until I was fit to be seen. Then I went out and caught the 7.45 bus."

There was a silence broken only by Miss Bennett's noisy sobs. "And Miss Roach was alive when you left?" Furnival asked.

"Oh, yes. She was glaring out of the window as I went down the drive."

"Well, if it's any consolation to you the figure wasn't priceless. Everyone was mistaken about that. But you've certainly caused a great deal of unnecessary work. For heaven's sake, why didn't you clear the business up when Miss Roach was dead? She couldn't get at you then."

"I don't know," Miss Bennett said miserably. "I felt so ashamed of being afraid to own up. It's degrading for one adult to be afraid of another. Then things sort of snowballed, there were so many policemen working on the case and it got harder and harder to tell the truth. And I suppose I was afraid, too, that you would think it gave me some sort of motive for killing Miss Roach."

"What did you do with the figure?" King asked. "Do you think after all this fuss we could have a look at him?"

"I kept the pieces," Miss Bennett said. She jumped up and fetched a large handbag from the sideboard. She felt around inside it until she came up with a buff envelope which she emptied gently on to one of Mrs. Milton's bright cushions. Furnival and King looked down at the half-dozen pieces of porcelain shining softly against the garish cloth. A tiny hand, lace ruffles at the wrist, a tan coat, a rose sprigged waistcoat, apple green breeches, and an exquisitely modelled head, the powdered wig held back by a velvet ribbon. Furnival picked up the base, the marks were identical with those he remembered on the base of the girl singer.

"I didn't know what to do with them," Miss Bennett explained. "I didn't like to throw them away. I had this queer feeling that although I hadn't harmed Miss Roach I was responsible for her death." She touched the tiny china head. "As though in some way he had set the whole thing rolling."

CHAPTER SEVENTEEN

IT WAS ten o'clock. Nothing further could usefully be done that night and Furnival felt too tired to think straight anyway. He remembered his advice to Cantwell and, with a brief good night to King, took himself home to bed.

Joanna was waiting for him in front of the fire. Without a word she fetched him coffee and sandwiches from the kitchen.

Furnival kissed her. "You're turning into a good dutiful wife in your old age."

Joanna poured the coffee. "We aim to please. Did you find the boy?"

"Sid? Yes, we found him."

"Was he all right?"

"He was fine. My hunch was correct. He'd gone to ground at his old school at Hunnington. The caretaker was looking after him."

"Well, isn't that good? You don't seem very pleased. I thought you were anxious to find him."

"Yes, it is good. I'm very relieved that he's turned up safe and sound. But now I've got to make some sense of it all. No more excuses now, everyone is available."

"Couldn't Sid advance your case at all?"

"He made a long statement, and Miss Bennett amended hers, but it doesn't seem to get us any further. The more information that comes in in this case the more of a puzzle it becomes."

"Is Sid innocent?"

"Oh, I think so. In fact that's exactly what he is—an innocent. So I'm left with Murphy, he would be the obvious candidate except for the fact that he has no motive, and I can't believe Miss Roach would have let him into the house if she could help it. Apart from Murphy there is only Shannon, Miss Bennett and, as a long shot, Laura Shannon."

"Surely Miss Bennett is a long shot, too? I've seen her picture in the paper, Matt. She looks such a timid little mouse."

"She looks even more of a timid mouse in the flesh, but the statistics show that murders are often committed by outwardly mousy types. Perhaps they are pushed beyond endurance. The fact is that Miss Bennett was on the spot and she was involved in a violent quarrel with Miss Roach. She also stands to benefit under Miss Roach's will, although I don't think that was the motive. It's a pretty strong case."

"Well, I hope it wasn't her," said Joanna firmly. "She deserves to enjoy herself after all those awful years with Miss Roach. What about George Shannon? He sounds a ghastly man."

"George has the all-consuming self-regard that is the hallmark of a certain type of killer. His hanky panky with those police records and the scheme to pinch his aunt's china figures indicate a moral sense that is shaky to say the least. Yes, he's certainly a possibility. I know Cantwell fancies him, but we've no concrete evidence against him."

"What is Sergeant Cantwell like?"

"He's a very good-looking young man," Furnival said. "I presume that is what you meant? Laura Shannon certainly seems to think so."

Joanna slid along the settee and rested her head on her husband's shoulder. "Well, maybe George will be found guilty, and we can fix Laura up with Sergeant Cantwell," she murmured sleepily.

"Sergeant Cantwell already has a wife. She's not my cup of tea, but apparently she has enough money to compensate. Also Laura Shannon would make a very bad policeman's wife, so stop talking like a woman's magazine."

"And how does one make a good policeman's wife?" Joanna murmured, planting light kisses on Furnival's left ear.

Furnival humped his wife off his shoulder and stood up. "Well, you could start by seeing that he got enough sleep!" he said.

He went upstairs while Joanna finished clearing away. He had a bath, hoping it would relax him, but he hadn't been in bed half an hour before he realised there was going to be little sleep for him that night. At first he fought against it, lying in the dark and trying to put the case and everyone connected with it out of his head. Twice he gave in and sat up, smoking a cigarette and trying to make some sense out of the thousands of words that churned around in his brain. About four o'clock he fell asleep at last, only to wake a couple of hours later conscious that some completely new idea was struggling to get through to him. He knew it was important, but he lay there feeling curiously detached, as though there was a giant sieve in his head riddling through all the irrelevant words and impressions and leaving exposed on the mesh of the sieve the undigestible lumps of truth.

Laura and Miss Bennett had both said that Miss Roach 'hardly ever had visitors', and he had ignored the possibility of someone being admitted to Rowan Lodge that night. Not an intruder, but someone expected, someone invited. He leant up on one elbow and stared bleakly into the darkness while he teased gingerly at the awful theory. Miss Bennett had said that Miss Roach had been angry with her principally 'for making her look a fool'. Furnival had never met Grace Roach but he did not think she was another Miss Bennett, too scared to own up to an error. Mrs. Robbins had said she was 'a fair and just woman'. She would know that the tramp would be hounded for stealing the figure Miss Bennett had broken.

Furnival suddenly felt icy cold, a score of words and actions, unnoticed until now, slipped smoothly into place. He said, "Oh, no!" in a voice so loud that Joanna stirred beside him. He switched on the bedside lamp and looked at the clock. It was almost six. Could he ring King? Emily King guarded her husband's sleep like a dragon, but he must speak to somebody. He dialled the number and after what seemed like an eternity King's voice came through.

"She would have called off the police," Furnival said. "She would have called Cantwell."

"Cantwell needn't have *gone* to Rowan Lodge," said King. "Even if Miss Roach had contacted him—and I'm inclined to agree she would have called him off as soon as possible, after her previous false alarms—there was no need for him to go to the house. They could have cleared it up over the phone." King was so offended by Furnival's implied slur on the Force that he found it hard to be civil.

They were sitting in Furnival's car outside King's house in the growing light of a very cold dawn. Furnival yawned and flexed his stiff face muscles.

" Cantwell said nothing about being called off," he said. " So Miss Roach never called him. Maybe she was going to, but she didn't have time. She was killed first."

" Then she must have been killed very early, because I feel strongly that she wouldn't have rested until she had called Cantwell. So in that case, who killed her? Shannon wasn't available to do the deed until eighty-forty, and Murphy is alibied until nine-thirty."

" You've got three or four good suspects, why look for another? And why Cantwell, for heaven's sake?"

" Oh, God, do you think I want to?" Furnival rubbed his eyes wearily. " I've been going over this for hours in my head. There was something about Cantwell. He was always there. I was amazed at his frantic energy. Frantic lest anything came up to implicate him? He had to be first to Sid Robbins—he almost drowned him—because he was terrified Robbins had seen something. He was so quick to find culprits—"

" Well, if he's going to be penalised for keenness!"

" No, listen, King. Cantwell is an intelligent man, but he'd have charged the milkman to find a culprit. Anyone would do."

" What about motive?" said King sulkily, " Or was it just a whim? Because she had wasted his time, perhaps?"

" That's what puzzled me," admitted Furnival. " There didn't seem to be any conceivable reason. Then I remembered the Chief saying something about there having been ' another ancient crime '."

King was silent. Then he said, " What are you going to do?"

" I'm going to do what I should have done a long time ago. I'm going to see Wainwright."

" Do we know where he lives?" King said.

" I rang the night desk. He lives on a small-holding four miles from Elmbridge."

They drove in silence, King stiff with disapproval, until, four miles short of Elmbridge, Furnival turned up a sign-posted lane that he had half-noticed on all his previous trips. After a couple of hundred yards they came to a cottage with leaded lancet windows rather like a Victorian gate lodge.

" I think this is the place," Furnival said. They parked the car on the grass verge and, hearing faint noises of activity, walked round to the back of the house. A plump, pleasant faced woman of about thirty was beating rugs against the wall. She jumped when she saw them.

" Oh, my, you did give me a turn! Did you want to see my Tom? He's just gone down the road with the churns."

" I expect it's your father I want to see," Furnival said. " Ex-sergeant Wainwright."

" That's right, that's Dad. But he's not up yet. He doesn't get up very early, there's not a lot for him to do around here."

" I'd appreciate it if you would call him. It's rather important. I'm Chief Inspector Furnival of Meddenham."

The woman invited them into a small font room where a smoky fire was struggling into life, and went upstairs to her father's room. They heard a brief muttered exchange, and a few minutes later heavy footsteps on the staircase. There was a good deal of noisy splashing from the kitchen, then Sergeant Wainwright appeared in the doorway.

He was an enormous man. Well over six feet in height, and probably weighing eighteen stone. He had a big amiable red face, glowing now from its vigorous splashing, and bright blue eyes. He wore a checked woollen dressing gown roped around his vast middle. He advanced into the room, seeming to fill it, and offered his hand to Furnival.

"Inspector Furnival? I've been half-expecting to see you."

"Why was that?"

"Why, over this Elmbridge business. I know Elmbridge like the back of my hand. Anything you want to know about Miss Roach or Miss Bennett, Georgie Shannon or Sid Robbins, you only have to ask me."

"I should have come to you sooner," Furnival said.

"Well, better late than never." Wainwright lowered his massive bulk into a chair. "We can have a nice chat now. I've told Betty to make us some tea."

"Have you any theories about the murder?" King asked respectfully.

Wainwright glowed. "There wasn't any trouble in Elmbridge when I was sergeant, I can tell you that," he said. "Nice law abiding class of people we had there then. I did have one little outburst from Sid Robbins, but personally I'd write him off for this job. He's got no murder in his heart. Now Georgie Shannon, he was an envious, discontented sort of lad. I know he didn't approve of his auntie buying that great big house for herself, and I suppose it was ridiculous in a way, but it was her dream all those years in that poky little shop . . ."

"Sergeant Wainwright, I don't have a lot of time,"

Furnival cut in firmly. "I really wanted you to tell me about the occasion when Miss Roach was attacked in her shop. Can you remember it?"

Wainwright looked surprised. "That was a long time ago. About ten years. But I remember it well. It was the worst case of that sort we ever had in Elmbridge. Miss Roach was badly hurt. She was always inclined to be suspicious after that." He scratched his great head. "Eh, it's funny she went that way in the end."

"What exactly happened? Did you get a statement from her?"

"Yes, I took a statement from her a few days after, when she wasn't quite so poorly. I remember it was a Friday night when it happened, just after eight o'clock. Miss Roach had closed the shop and she was cashing up, when there was a tap at the door. She opened the door a crack and the young man outside asked her to sell him some cigarettes. She let him in and locked the door behind him. As she turned her back on him to walk over to the counter he coshed her and she went out like a light. Fractured her skull. The copper on the beat spotted her two hours later. The till had been emptied, about thirty pounds had gone."

"Did she get a look at the man?" Furnival asked. As he waited for Wainwright's answer he was conscious of holding his breath.

"Yes she did. She didn't know him, of course, he was a stranger, but I remember she said he 'had a nice face', that's why she didn't hesitate to open up for him. He was about eighteen years old, with a nice lively face, and, oh yes, she said he had bright red hair."

CHAPTER EIGHTEEN

AT ABOUT the same time as Furnival and King were rousing Sergeant Wainwright, Laura Shannon was reluctantly preparing to rise from her bed. It was barely eight o'clock, but George had already departed for Rowan Lodge to continue sorting Aunt Grace's possessions with an enthusiasm which, only one day after the funeral, Laura thought scarcely decent.

She sat up in bed and drank the cooling cup of tea he had left by her bedside. There was no doubt that George had been more thoughtful towards her in the last few days. When she had finished her tea she was tempted to slide beneath the covers again, but the noise from the children, of which she had been dimly aware for some time, had grown too loud to be ignored. With a muttered curse Laura stumbled out of bed, pulled on a sweater and slacks, and hurried downstairs.

She soon located the noise as coming through the steel door from the cell block. Apart from the danger of the children managing to lock themselves in the cells, (tempting, thought Laura fleetingly), that part of the house was icy cold and she made haste to evict them.

The altercation seemed to be centred on Martin's big wooden truck. Still clad only in pyjamas he was spread-eagled across it roaring lustily, while Judy in vest and knickers was attempting to dislodge him with fists, feet and fingernails.

"*Judy*!" Laura shrieked. "You naughty girl! Leave Martin alone. That is his truck, and you shouldn't kick and scratch anyway. He's only a baby."

"But Mummy, he's got my *papers*," Judy sat back on the floor, tears of frustration streaming down her face. "He took my papers and he's put them in his van."

"Paper van," explained Martin, beaming at his mother. "Paper van. Bang!" He crashed the van as hard as he could against the wall, dislodging a shower of plaster.

"*Martin*, stop doing that!" Laura knelt beside the van. "What have you got in there? If it's the Sunday paper you mustn't make a mess of it before Daddy has seen it."

"Not *newspapers*," sobbed Judy. "*Office* papers. I found them and I was playing Daddy's office with them."

"Let me see." Laura opened the back door of the truck and pulled out a tightly crammed wedge of papers. Glancing at them she realised immediately what they must be. "These are the police papers Mr. Cantwell was looking for. Where did you find them, Judy?"

"In a cupboard in the office. I've had them for ages. I hid them in my doll's house in case Martin got them."

"Well, I'm sorry, darling, but neither of you can play with them. They belong to the police and I must telephone Mr. Cantwell to come and collect them. But when you've washed and dressed and eaten your breakfast, and *if* you stop quarrelling, you can have some old magazines, Martin, and Judy can have some writing paper."

Laura hauled the two of them, momentarily appeased, back upstairs, washed and dressed them, and settled them at the kitchen table with bowls of cereal. She felt an illicit little thrill of pleasure at the thought of Cantwell's visit, and she took time to make up her face and tidy her hair before she called the station. She was disappointed to learn that Cantwell was not in the office, but the officer on duty assured her that he would pass on her message as soon as he arrived. The schoolgirl who occasionally minded the children called to take them to the park and Laura put on their coats and waved them thankfully off.

She picked up the crumpled pile of statements and carried them into the front room where she attempted to smooth out some of the creases. She wondered what had fascinated George about the documents, she knew that Furnival had been angry with him for not giving them up. She picked up the topmost paper and started idly to read it.

Half an hour later Laura was still absorbed. The statements were just about the most interesting reading matter that had ever come her way. No wonder George had hung on to them! Her eyes grew wider as she read. This was quite a different Elmbridge from the one she knew and hated. Here was Miss Wittering of all people claiming indecent assault by a Major Astley, a gentleman whom Laura did not know and who, in fact, had died of relief shortly after the case had failed. Another similar case involved the dehydrated manageress of the local baby linen shop. Here were several drunken driving charges, among them one against the bank manager who always treated Laura so snootily.

She pawed through the remaining pile of papers. There would not be time to read them all, Sergeant Cantwell would be here at any minute, yet who knew what goodies she might be missing? As Laura neared the bottom of the pile the name Grace Roach seemed to leap from the page at her. She pulled out the sheet and read the preamble. Why, it was the attack on Aunt Grace in her shop all those years ago. She started to read the statement with only mild interest. It was quite a brief report and Laura finished it without reaction. Then a second later, like the afterwash of a great ship engulfing a small craft, a feeling of icy cold crept over her and her scalp froze. She read the end of the statement again. She was too riveted to hear the knock at the front door, or to hear it opened and the steps along the hall. She did not look up until he was in the room. She knew she must look at him in the same silly flirtatious manner that she had before, but she could not. She could only stare at him in terror. Cantwell looked at the papers spread over the table and then at her. He walked round the table and stood behind her reading Miss Roach's statement. She could feel his body against her back. She was paralyzed with fear. She heard herself croak, "It was you. It was you."

Cantwell put his warm hand on her shoulder close to her throat. "Oh, Laura, it was so long ago. It was such bloody bad luck. I barely recognised her. Even after I had talked to her for half an hour I wasn't sure it was the same woman. I didn't think she recognised me, she gave no sign. But at night when she sent for me to come back—" His voice choked. "She sat in that chair and folded her hands so smug, and she said that she had realised I was that boy. She was going to turn me in. What else could I do?"

"She was an old lady," whispered Laura.

"Yes, she was old, she'd had her life. Mine was to come. I had so much to lose, Laura—" He moved his hand gently on her shoulder, and his movement somehow freed her limbs into panicky motion. She half fell out of the chair and stumbled across the room to the door. Cantwell was after her in a flash, no longer regretful, but decisive and murderous. Laura saw the steel door to the cell block still open in front of her. She dashed through it, but Cantwell was too close on her heels for her to shut the door on him. She fell back into the nearest cell and with a sob of relief slammed the door shut and heard the great lock engage. Cantwell's face appeared at the open grill, dead white, his eyes blazing, his usual pleasant expression contorted with desperation. Laura backed away from him to the farthest corner. She scrambled up on to the bunk until her face was near the high small window. "George!" she screamed. "Oh, George, George!"

Just about the time that Laura Shannon was savouring Major Astley's indiscretions with Miss Wittering, Furnival and King emerged from Wainwright's cottage.

"You've still no proof," King was saying stubbornly. "Thousands of chaps have bright red hair."

"The age is right."

They got into the car but Furnival did not start the engine.

"What's your idea?" King persisted. "Miss Roach wasn't sure of him on the morning visit and asked him to come again in person to make sure?"

"Something like that. Maybe she knew his face but simply couldn't believe it. After all a policeman. The black and the white, hare and hounds, would be so separate for her."

"She wouldn't have let him in."

"I think she would. I think that robbery still festered so much she would have forgotten all caution to unmask her attacker. And perhaps she was still not certain."

King tried again. "Cantwell wouldn't have risked settling here."

"He had to. He didn't want to, but he had no choice. His wife and his wealthy in-laws dictated the terms. I suppose when he saw that Miss Roach's shop was demolished he thought it was worth the risk. She could have been dead by now, she was over seventy." Furnival started the car and they coasted down to the main road. "Think of the break-in at the Shannons," he said. "Those old reports had been lying around the place unmolested for years until Cantwell learned they were there. Who knew Laura Shannon would be out that day? She was always at home, it was one of her complaints. But Cantwell knew, because his wife had told him. Remember how eager he was to get his hands on those records? How he crammed them into his case before we could get a look at them? Can you think of any explanation that covers that break-in better?"

King was silent for a moment, then he said quietly, "No. No, I can't. What will you do?"

Furnival was listening to other voices, voices that had gone unheard because they seemed to have no relevance. "He's very ambitious, his in-laws like him to move in the right circles," and, right at the very beginning, "it's a good thing Elmbridge waited for him to come along to have its first murder." He trod on the accelerator. "We've got to find that statement Miss Roach made at the time of her attack," he said. "It may be the only evidence there is against him."

In a few minutes the straggling outskirts of Elmbridge

came into view. Just short of the police station Furnival slowed down and let King out. " If Cantwell is there keep him talking on some pretext, but for God's sake don't let him suspect anything. I'll take the old Station House apart looking for that statement. If I find it I'll get back to Meddenham and confer with the Chief."

" He's going to love you for this," said King lugubriously. " Suppose Cantwell found the statement when he broke in?"

" Then we haven't a hope," said Furnival. He slammed the car door and drove on to the Shannons. He parked the car beside the house and knocked at the front door. When his knocking was unanswered he tried the door handle. It was locked. Furnival swore. He was so keyed up to finding the statement that he could not bear to be baulked. He hurried up the narrow alley that led to the back of the house; perhaps he could get in that way. He emerged from the alley literally on the river bank. The old station yard was surrounded by a shoulder high brick wall, but it was too far decayed to present any obstacle. Furnival scrambled up a mound of fallen masonry and through one of the larger gaps. He landed in a small yard deep in weeds and rank grass and dotted with broken toys. In front of him he saw the back wall of the house, the broken window beside the door, the narrow barred windows of the two cells. And at one cell window, the golden head and clutching hands and terrified eyes of Laura Shannon.

Furnival crossed the yard in six strides. He guessed from Laura's contorted face that she was screaming at full lung power, but her voice came only faintly through the thick glass, " Sergeant Cantwell. Outside the door. He's trying to kill me!"

Furnival ran to the back door of the house, slowed down, and pushed it open cautiously. Just inside the passage was the kitchen door, and further down, near the front of the house, the doors of the dining-room and the lounge. Between the two was the heavy steel door to the cell block. All the doors stood open. The house was deathly quiet. He crept forward, checking the kitchen as he passed. He pushed the steel door wider. He could see the short dark passage, the two cell doors, the foot of the narrow staircase. Ahead of him the second steel door that barred the end of the passage was securely shut. There was no sign of Cantwell. He crossed to Laura's cell. "All right, open up, it's me, Mrs. Shannon." He heard her sobbing as she struggled with the lock. She got the door open at last and fell into his arms with a loud wail. Then there was a tremendous shove between his shoulder blades and he pitched forward into the cell on top of Laura Shannon.

They picked themselves up and Furnival spun round to the door. They could hear Cantwell's feet running down the passage to the front door. "Damn and blast!" Furnival yelled. "He must have been hiding in the second cell." He rattled the cell door helplessly. "And he's bolted this bloody thing!" He looked up at the window. "Is there something we can smash the glass with?" Laura looked round and picked up Martin's truck that was still lying on the floor. Furnival managed to insert it between the bars and started to bang at the window, but the narrow space and the angle made it difficult to get any force behind the blows. "What made him go for you?" he asked Laura.

"I found the statement Aunt Grace made when she was attacked. It said that her attacker was nice looking with bright red hair. Sergeant Cantwell sprang to my mind immediately. As I was reading it he walked in. I suppose he saw my face."

Furnival squeezed her shoulder to silence her. He had frozen into immobility, the truck still upraised in his hand. Laura followed his gaze. Through the little window they could see the centre arch of the bridge. For once it was deserted. They saw Cantwell clamber over the parapet and cling for a moment to the outside before he dropped to the water below. They saw his bright hair flash once in the sun before the swirling brown water closed over it. Laura and Furnival stared hypnotised at the spot, but he did not reappear.

"Surely he could swim," Laura whispered.

"Yes," said Furnival. "He could." He started to hammer on the window again, but they heard a loud clanging from the corridor outside the cell, and in a minute King appeared in the doorway.

"You'll never live this down, Chief!" he grinned. Then he caught their expression and sobered rapidly.

"Cantwell's in the river," Furnival said.

The next few hours were a nightmare. Repeated diving in the turbulent water revealed nothing, and in the afternoon the dragging tackle that had been standing by for Sid Robbins was brought in. Just as it grew dusk Cantwell's body came to the surface only twenty yards from the bridge.

At midnight Furnival sat in his office with King, Superintendent Peters, and the Chief Constable. The miserable preliminaries had been cleared away, but all the men felt a reluctance to go home. An air of deep gloom hung over the room.

"As he said to Laura Shannon. 'It was such bloody bad

luck,' " Furnival said. " He never associated the old woman in the little shop with the lady in the big house. She was the last person he expected to see."

" I don't understand why he brought us in," King said. " He could have tried to pass her death off as an accident. It was quite feasible."

" He wasn't really responsible for us being called in, although he tried to give that impression," said Furnival. " Miss Bennett said to me, 'I told Sergeant Cantwell to ring you.' He couldn't refuse without making her suspicious."

" How did his wife take it?" Daneman asked.

Furnival shrugged. " She showed no sign of grief. She just packed up her clothes and moved back to her parents' house. She has verified that Cantwell was out between eight and nine o'clock on Monday night, so, as I thought, Miss Roach must have telephoned him as soon as Miss Bennett left the house."

" He was such a promising copper," Peters groaned, not for the first time.

" He was the best cadet of his year," said Daneman. " We should have a P.R.O. to handle this one. How does a brutal young thug turn into the best police cadet of the year?"

" By excellence, the same as any other," Furnival said. " He was a good man with a fissure of unbalance."

The men were silent. " You've let Murphy out?" Daneman asked.

" Yes. He was quite reluctant to go. Winter is setting in," said Furnival. " Incidentally, there was one cheering note this evening. Bill Kennedy rang me from Hunnington. He's talked his principal into taking Sid Robbins on as his assistant." He looked at Peters' and Daneman's bleak faces and saw that they were hardly cheered. "It seemed like a good solution for Robbins," he finished lamely.

There was another pause. "Did we find out what Shannon did with his lost forty minutes?" Peters asked.

"Yes, he told me he was driving around trying to decide what to do about the two women in his life!" said Furnival. "Whether to finish with Gwen, or make a clean breast of it to Laura. I gather Laura won. He told me, too, how his aunt came to buy Rowan Lodge. She had set her heart on a big country house, and she looked at a lot to find the perfect place. Some of the others were more suitable, but it was the rowan trees that decided her. She had just had that attack, and she was a bit superstitious, and she reckoned that rowan trees kept away evil!"

"Yes, that's been a common folk belief for centuries in all parts of Britain and Scandinavia," Daneman said. "You carried a piece in your hand on May Day when the witches and fairies were about. You hung the hearth and the barns with it. In Cornwall a piece in your pocket averted ill-wishing. Nowadays, you just plant them around the house. Its power was generally suppose to come from the colour of its berries, there was no better colour against evil than red. An ancient verse goes,

> 'Roan-tree and red thread
> Hold the witches a' in dread.'

However, in my opinion—"

King yawned across the lecture. "And in my opinion," he said as he prepared to take his leave. "It doesn't bloody work."